ten miles past normal

normal

ten miles past

frances o'roark dowell

ATHENEUM BOOKS FOR YOUNG READERS
New York London Toronto Sydney

ATHENEUM BOOKS FOR YOUNG READERS
An imprint of Simon & Schuster Children's Publishing Division
1230 Avenue of the Americas, New York, New York 10020

Book design by Debra Sfetsios-Conover
The text for this book is set in Scala and Scala Hans.
Manufactured in the United States of America
First Edition
10 9 8 7 6 5 4 3 2 1
Library of Congress Cataloging-in-Publication Data
Dowell, Frances O'Roark.
Ten miles past normal / Frances O'Roark Dowell. — 1st ed.
p. cm.
Summary: Because living with "modern-hippy" parents on a goat farm means fourteen-year-old Janie Gorman cannot have a normal high school life, she tries joining Jam Band, making friends with Monster, and spending time with elderly former Civil Rights workers.
ISBN 978-1-4169-9585-2
[1. Farm life—North Carolina—Fiction. 2. Interpersonal relations—Fiction. 3. High schools—Fiction. 4. Schools—Fiction. 5. Bands (Music)—Fiction. 6. Civil rights movements—Fiction. 7. North Carolina—Fiction.] I. Title.
PZ7.D75455Ten 2011
[Fic]—dc22
2010022041
ISBN 978-1-4169-9587-6 (eBook)

For Amy Graham and Danielle Paul—

high school would have been so much cooler with you guys along for the ride.

Acknowledgments

The author would like to thank Caitlyn Dlouhy and Kiley Frank; as always, they did most of the heavy lifting. She greatly appreciates Alison Velea and Valerie Shea, who made the copyediting process a joy, and Debra Sfetsios-Conover and Elizabeth Blake-Linn, for making the book look so beautiful. She is eternally grateful to Clifton, Jack, and Will Dowell, and to Travis, the best dog ever. She owes a debt of gratitude to Jenna Woginrich, whose book *Made from Scratch* inspired her to take up the fiddle and to write a book with chickens and goats in it.

Finally, the author would like to go on record as saying that if she ever ends up down on the farm, it will be thanks to Wendell Berry, who, as far as the author is concerned, rocks.

You're all invited to the hootenanny.

Chapter One

More Tales of the Amazing Farm Girl

No one can figure out where the terrible smell is coming from, but everyone on the bus this morning can smell it and has an opinion.

"Dude, I bet we just ran over a skunk!" yells out Stoner Guy No. 1 from the back of the bus. "That happened to us when I was a kid. We had to get rid of our car, 'cause the smell was, like, permanent."

"No way, dude," comes the reply from his compadre, Stoner Guy No. 2. "That's not skunk. That is definitely fecund matter we're smelling."

"*Fecal*, dude, *fecal*," Stoner Guy No. 1 corrects him.

"That's what I'm saying, dude."

As it turns out, what we're smelling is my shoe. Or, more to the point, the fecund matter that has attached itself to my shoe.

Goat poop.

The general din that erupts around me when the source of the terrible smell is traced to my left foot mostly consists of hooting, jeering, and a collective plea for me to throw the offending ballet flat out the window.

"No throwing anything from the windows," Steve, our bus driver, yells out from the front. "I don't care how bad it stinks."

All the kids sitting near me move to the back of the bus, cramming in three and even four to a seat, so I'm sitting alone in a sea of empty rows. Not just my face, but my whole body, has turned hot lava red.

Farm Girl strikes again.

I mentally retrace my smelly steps to the bus stop, back down the driveway to the house, in through the front door, out through the back door, and all the way to the goat pen. Milking the goats every morning is the first chore of my day, and on school days, when I'm running late, I sometimes risk wearing my civilian clothes, careful not to squirt or spill any goat milk on my jeans, and very, very careful to avoid the fragrant goat poop pellets.

This morning I was running later than usual and milked the girls at warp speed. I recall being proud not to have gotten any milk on myself or even on the ground. Clearly I should have focused less on the goats' milk and more on their other bodily excretions.

As soon as the bus pulls up to school, I make my escape

and sprint to the girls' bathroom on the second floor by the art room, hoping it won't be as populated as the more conveniently located first-floor bathroom. I find two girls huddled by the radiator grille, one crying, the other comforting her. They appear to be the only people in here. The comforter glares at me for invading their space, and I smile back lamely, holding up my shoe.

"Unfortunate incident," I explain, sounding possibly even dumber than I feel. "Just ignore me."

The sobbing girl sniffs the air and gasps, "What's that smell?"

I grab a wad of paper towels from the dispenser. "My shoe. Sorry. I stepped in some goat poop this morning. It must have been really fresh, too, because usually goat manure doesn't stink that much. The pellets are generally pretty dry."

Sobbing Girl's eyes widen in recognition. "Aren't you in my PE class? Didn't you, like, one time have this horrible rash on your legs? From hay or something?"

"It was actually this organic fertilizer my dad was trying," I explain, trying to pretend we're having a perfectly normal teenage girl conversation. "Turns out I'm allergic to worm castings. But I'm not actually allergic to worms. Go figure."

The girls stare at each other a second and crack up. "Wow!" Sobbing Girl says. "That's the most insane thing anyone has ever said to me! You are totally weird."

Gosh, I'm glad I could cheer her up.

The girls leave, still giggling, and I scrub my shoe until there is only the faintest whiff of goat matter left. I slip the shoe on my foot, grab my backpack, and hurry out the bathroom toward my locker, eyes downward. With any luck, nobody from my bus will be around, and if they are, they won't notice me.

"Nice shoes!" someone yells out from a group of jocks huddled around a locker. "You oughta bottle that smell. Eau de Crap!"

I breathe in deeply through my nose, an exercise I read about in my best friend Sarah's yoga magazine. Breathe in, focus deeply on an image you find pleasing and relaxing, breathe out.

My rebel brain immediately envisions the farm on a summer morning, the air already hazy, butterflies floating across the wildflowers. I see the house with its wraparound porch, fresh white paint, cerulean blue shutters. I hear the slam of a screen door, the peaceful clucking of chickens.

Ah, yes, our farm. How relaxing to meditate on the place that has made me the laughingstock of the ninth grade and probably the biggest loser in the entire school.

And to think it was my idea to live there in the first place.

Chapter Two

A Brief History of How I Ruined My Own Life

Like all fourteen-year-olds, I used to be a nine-year-old. In retrospect, I was an annoyingly perky and enthusiastic nine-year-old. In fact, I've been enthusiastic my entire life, up until this fall, when high school sucked every last ounce of enthusiasm right out of me.

For the big fourth-grade field trip that year, we rode in a rattling yellow school bus out to the country to visit an organic farm. The farmers were a young couple with a baby, a flock of chickens, and four goats. They talked a lot about growing vegetables in an environmentally friendly way and evil factory farms where the cows were very, very unhappy. What I liked about the field trip was the goat cheese and the homemade bread the farmers served after we finished touring their farm. I remember having some sort of profound thought like, "Boy, farmers sure do eat good," and suddenly my mind was made up: I wanted to live on a farm for the rest of my life.

Like I said, I was an enthusiastic kid. I was always coming up with new ideas—Let's keep a horse in the backyard! Let's adopt a homeless person!—and my parents were always rejecting them. So when I suggested we'd all be happier on a farm raising goats and baking bread, well, I meant it, but I didn't expect to be taken seriously.

We were sitting at the dinner table, eating a Stouffer's frozen lasagna that hadn't quite gotten heated all the way through ("Think of it as lasagna sorbet," my mother suggested, and I was so young and enthusiastic at the time that I actually tried to think of it that way), when I told my parents we should move to a farm and raise goats. I listed the many benefits of this plan (free goat cheese being number one on the list; I forget now what number two was) and sat back, waiting to be rejected yet again.

But instead of shaking her head and saying, "I'm sorry, Janie, but I just don't think that's going to work for us as a family right now" (which is what she said about the horse and the homeless person), my mother got very quiet. She looked at my father, her eyes sort of glimmering, a dreamy expression on her face.

"Daddy and I used to talk about living on a farm all the time," she said after a moment. "Didn't we, honey?"

"Before we had kids," my dad agreed. "Back before life got so crazy."

"Life wouldn't be crazy on a farm," I insisted. "It's very peaceful on a farm."

I had no idea what I was talking about. My farm experience consisted of one field trip and approximately two hundred picture books about Old MacDonald and Chicken Little and cows that typed. But clearly my suggestion struck a chord with my parents, who started talking about how great it would be to get out of the suburbs, to grow our own food, to raise chickens and have fresh eggs every day.

"You guys could quit your jobs," I told them. "You could be outside in the fresh air. It would be good for your health!"

"Well, I don't think we could quit our jobs, cowgirl," my dad said. "In fact, I don't want to quit my job. But it might be nice to live farther out in the country."

I sat back in my seat, dazed. My parents were actually taking one of my ideas seriously! It made me feel important, almost grown-up.

"It's a wonderful idea, Janie," my mom declared.

My dad grinned at me. "A humdinger of an idea."

Now, it did occur to me that if we lived on a farm, my best friend, Sarah, would no longer live across the street. Megan Grant, who had spent the last four months trying to steal Sarah away from me, would have full access to her while I'd be out collecting eggs in the countryside. Alone. By myself.

On the other hand, maybe my parents would finally get me a horse.

Bonus.

"Well, if you guys think so," I said modestly. "I do think farms are nice. Especially farms with stables."

Eight months later, we were farmers. I remember the day we moved out to the farm, the excitement I felt as I ran like a maniac up and down the stairs of the farm house, built circa 1892, with its windows that rattled with every breeze and broad oak floors that groaned in the middle of cold winter nights. I was Laura Ingalls Wilder, Anne of Green Gables; I was a girl who lived on a farm. Outside, the honeysuckle was just beginning to bloom and the whole world smelled sweet.

And the kids at school? They thought it was cool we'd moved to a farm. We had the fifth-grade end-of-the-year party out by our pond, and the sixth-grade fall festival took place in the barn. Being Farm Girl meant social bonus points.

High school changed all of that. For one thing, no one I met in high school had fond memories of hanging out in our barnyard and feeding corn to the chickens. For another, no one thought it was cute that half the time I smelled like the barn I spent the first thirty minutes of my morning in.

They thought it was weird. They thought I was weird.

And suddenly I realized that living on a farm *was* weird. Milking goats and pushing a chickenmobile around the yard every morning, dumping eggshells and coffee grounds into the composter every night after the dishes were done. Knowing way too much about manure and fertilizers and the organic way to grow bok choy. What kind of normal teenage girl lived this way?

The people at school were right—I was weird.

And I only had myself to blame.

Chapter Three

Meanwhile,
Back at the Ranch . . .

Saturday morning I'm awakened at an absurdly early hour by Ty Cobb, our rooster, who doesn't know from weekends. Every day is a day to get up with the sun, in Ty Cobb's opinion.

"I think Ty Cobb would taste good for lunch, don't you?" I ask my dad when we meet in the hallway, both of us yawning. "You can eat roosters, you know. Some people have rooster for Thanksgiving instead of turkey."

My father heads downstairs. "We need Ty Cobb. Without him, we don't get baby chicks. You like chicks, remember?"

I clomp down the staircase after him. "No, that's Avery who likes baby chicks. Or at least she likes flushing them down the toilet."

I learned very early in my farming career not to get too attached to the smaller animals. There are always predators like Avery around who will break your heart by flushing away the livestock.

"That was years ago," my dad points out. "I can't even think of the last time Avery put a chick in the toilet."

"Dad, we've only lived here five years. It's not ancient history."

We arrive in the kitchen, where my mom and my eight-year-old sister, Avery, are digging into their scrambled eggs. Farm-fresh scrambled eggs, my mom would be the first person to point out.

I would be the first person to point out that we don't actually live on a farm. It's more like a farm-ette. A mini-farm. No, make that a wannabe farm.

I am the only person in my family who has these sorts of thoughts.

"Avery and I are going to the flea market after chores this morning," my mom informs me at breakfast. "Do you want to come?"

"I'm going to go to Sarah's," I say, pouring myself some juice, my tone making it clear that even if I had no plans, my answer would be *Not a chance*. "We've got work to do on our project."

"I need your help this afternoon, don't forget." My father is standing in the doorway, coffee mug in hand, about to head out back. "It's Mr. Pritchard today."

I sigh but make an honest effort not to roll my eyes.

"Okay. But can we not stay out there all afternoon?"

"I thought you liked Mr. Pritchard." My dad sounds vaguely hurt, like he can't understand why I'm not doing cartwheels at the thought of spending yet another weekend afternoon helping him gather data for his latest academic adventure.

"I do, but the last time we went to see him, we were there for, like, five hours."

"He's a fascinating old guy." My dad grabs his pink Al's Garage cap from its peg and shoves it on his head. "And he won't be around forever."

I have to admit this is true. We've gone to visit Mr. Pritchard four times now, and each time he's seemed a little bit smaller. It's possible that one day he'll simply disappear into thin air and never be heard from again.

After breakfast, I pull on my Official Farming Jeans, which are jeans that are never worn for anything else but outdoor chores, so I don't worry about what kind of muck gets on them. In fact, I hardly ever wash them, because why bother? It's true they've developed a distinct odor that even Avery, Miss "I'll Take a Bath Once a Month, but Only If Absolutely Necessary," wrinkles her nose at, but to me that's the point. If you're going to give me chores that result in goat poop on my pants, you're going to pay the olfactory price.

Next, I don my Official Farming Shirt, a blue plaid

flannel shirt missing the bottom two buttons, which I wear over the "Rednecks for Peace" T-shirt my dad gave me for Christmas last year. He keeps asking me why I don't wear the T-shirt so everyone can see it, and my answer is pretty simple: I'm not a redneck. I'm not a rural person, a country girl, or just plain folks. I'm doing my best to be a normal teenage girl here, people. That I'm for peace is entirely beside the point.

In the mudroom, I pull on my work boots, which are brown and lace up to mid-shin and could not be uglier. But when you're stomping around in the mud, pretty footwear isn't exactly a priority. In fact, as I learned so well yesterday, it should be avoided at all costs.

Now it's time to enter Farm World with my mental mixed bag of feelings. The farm is beautiful! (It smells.) It's natural! (It makes me smell, naturally.) It's environmentally friendly! (It's an environment that produces teenage girls who are shunned by their peers for smelling like their environment.)

"You used to love it here," my mom says now when I complain about living miles away from civilizing influences, such as shopping malls and best friends. "You used to say living on a farm was the best thing ever."

"That was back when I was a kid," I point out. "I've matured."

"Isn't there anything you still like about it?"

My mom always looks so disappointed when she asks this. In fact, "confused disappointment" seems to be my parents' number one reaction to me these days. Sarah says it could be worse. According to Sarah, her parents' reactions to her plans and ideas could best be described as "shocked disapproval." And it's true, the Lymans can be pretty strict, but at least they don't act like everything Sarah says and does is an indictment of their chosen lifestyle.

"It's pretty," I admit. "And you make great bread."

My mom is a master baker. If you'd known her before we moved out here, you'd be flabbergasted to hear this. I mean, she was almost famous for how bad her cooking was. Who could forget the elementary school PTA bake sale in third grade, when my mom sent in a batch of chocolate-chip cookies? I handed the shoebox full of cookies over to one of the PTA moms, who chirped, "Oh, chocolate chip, my favorite!" then winked at me and whispered, "I'm going to sneak one. Don't tell!"

She snuck, she bit, she tasted, she spat. After she recovered, she put the box under the table and smiled weakly at me. "Maybe we'll just save these for later."

For the most part, my mom didn't bake, and she didn't cook. She bought, and she thawed and reheated. She did a truckload of microwaving. But once we moved to the country, she decided to take her cooking and baking seriously. "I want to live a homemade life," she declared, and it only took her a couple of months to figure out that baking soda was not a substitute for baking powder and that following a recipe without skipping any steps, even the boring ones, was a good thing.

So that was a definite plus side to farm life—edible cooking.

Sometimes I feel guilty that I don't love the farm the way I used to. It's the kind of guilt you feel when you stop hanging out with a friend you don't have anything in common with anymore. You think she's great, but there's nothing to talk about. She's into soccer, you're into basketball. She likes partying, you're a library girl. She's all about crop rotation, you're all about not being completely humiliated walking down the halls of your high school because manure's clinging to your shoes.

When I get out to the goat pen, the girls await. Loretta Lynn trots up to greet me, rubbing her nose against my arm. She, like her boon companions Patsy Cline and Kitty Wells, is a Nubian, which means she has a very nice Roman nose and doesn't look like a picture-book goat at all. Of all the girls, she's the most affectionate. That's probably because she's at the bottom of the goat hierarchy. Loretta Lynn is sort of like Andie Rowan in eighth grade, who was nice to everyone in hopes that one day someone would actually say hi to her in the hallway.

In one hand I carry a bucket, in the other, a stool. After

four years of goat milking, I'm pretty much an expert at it, but unlike when I was ten, when I could say the word "teat" without blushing, now I can't even think the word "teat" without dying a little death. But aside from the unfortunate vocabulary aspect of it, I actually like milking the goats. It's satisfying to fill up a bucket with milk that later will become delicious, creamy cheese.

I've also found that milking goats can be therapeutic. I talk to the girls to calm them, and because I need a topic to talk about, and because they don't really care what that topic is, usually I talk about myself. Really, they seem pretty interested, which is amazing, given how truly mundane my personal life is.

"So Sarah and I already got started on our project—total shock, since it's not even due until November—but it looks like we're going to have to change the whole thing, since Katie Womack and Lindsey Holpe claim they signed up to do Madeleine Albright before we did. Total lie, by the way, but Ms. Morrison is so clueless, it's pathetic. Also, she and Katie Womack's mom went to college together or something, so Katie can do whatever she wants as far as Ms. Morrison is concerned."

Loretta Lynn looks at me sympathetically over her shoulder, and I continue happily. It's amazing how fun it is to just say whatever comes to your mind and not worry that everyone will think you're a total idiot.

"Mom thinks we should do a project on Sally Ride, which would be okay, except I'm not that interested in space travel, and neither is Sarah. Wouldn't it be sort of disrespectful to be so totally, well, unenthusiastic?"

Loretta Lynn shifts her weight around, the way you would while sitting through a really long lecture on, say, the Peruvian Bill of Rights. Is it possible she's getting bored? Okay, so this is maybe the third time we've had this discussion, but still, she's a goat. A bottom-of-the-pecking-order goat.

"Well, I'm sorry," I tell her after a moment or two of petulant silence on my part. "But we've got to pick a project topic, and we need to do it this afternoon to turn in on Monday, and if I don't come up with a totally awesome topic, you know what Sarah's going to want to do, don't you? You know what completely stale idea she's going to suggest, right?"

Loretta Lynn settles. She loves it when I talk trash about Sarah.

"Let's say it all together on the count of three—one . . . two . . . three . . . Geraldine Ferraro!"

Loretta Lynn bleats an exclamation of pure dismay. *The first woman vice-presidential candidate, who ran with Walter Mondale in 1984?* she seems to be asking. *That Geraldine Ferraro?*

"Yes," I affirm. "*That* Geraldine Ferraro."

Sarah Lyman has been my best friend since the summer before first grade, when we both moved to Victoria Lane on the exact same day, our houses directly across the street from each other. As soon as Sarah saw me sitting on my front step, she ran over to me yelling, "Are you the first-grade girl they promised me?"

"Who promised you?" I looked at the tiny girl standing in front me, her yellow braids tied with red and white polka-dot ribbons, and was sure she couldn't possibly be going into first grade. Maybe someone was promising the preschool girls in the neighborhood a free elementary school student if they ate their peas five nights in a row.

But no. "I'm Sarah," she said, offering me her tiny hand. "I'm in first grade too. So we should probably be best friends and share things. I have a big sister named Emma, but she won't share anything."

Sarah and I have shared a lot over the years—clothes, books, earrings, a love of trashy magazines, a dedicated passion for funky shoes, and an abiding belief that there exists somewhere an island of cute, smart boys who are interested in girls for their minds. We've yet to find this magical land, but we haven't given up hope.

This past summer Sarah picked up a copy of the *Atlantic* in her dentist's office and read a horrifying account of child slave labor in the cocoa fields of Ghana. Sarah lives for chocolate, but now she can't bring herself to eat it.

Solution? Become the U.S. ambassador to Ghana and convert cocoa production into a democratic, humane, and child-friendly industry we can all feel good about.

"I'd already been considering a career in politics," she explained to me at the pool soon after her decision was made. "And you know how I feel about chocolate."

In preparation for her ambassadorship, Sarah signed up for the Great Girls and Women of American History elective, and I signed up too, so we'd have at least one class together. Sarah's hoping to pick up some helpful hints by studying famous women politicians such as Hilary Rodham Clinton, Nancy Pelosi, and, of course, Geraldine Ferraro, former vice-presidential candidate *and* onetime U.S. ambassador to the United Nations Commission on Human Rights.

After I finish with the milking, get the girls fed, and freshen their water, it's off to make myself presentable for what I've come to think of as the Real World. When you live in Farm World—or in our case, Mini-Farm World, a land of five acres, a flock of chickens, and one small goat herd—smelly jeans and muddy boots are perfectly acceptable. But in the Real World, a little more effort is expected.

"I'm going to Sarah's," I yell to my dad from the back porch after I've showered and put on jeans that don't stink to high heaven. He's fixing a wheel on the chicken tractor, the mobile coop our flock lives in. "I guess you don't have time to give me a ride, do you?"

My dad shakes his head. "Sorry. Too much work to do. Be back by one, okay?"

"Okay," I yell, then head out back, where my trusty bike is leaning against the side of the garage. As I begin my ride down the gravel driveway, I pretend I'm actually riding a moped through the Italian countryside, and in a matter of moments I'll be in the center of Venice, where I'll meet my charming and fashionable friends for espresso and gossip.

By the time I've turned left onto Haw River Road, I've forgotten that Farm World even exists.

Chapter Four

The Bus Ride of Doom

The bus picks me up Monday at the end of our driveway, the same way it does every morning, only on this particular Monday morning I have triple-checked my shoes for problem odors. I'm the first passenger and have my pick of seats. In my opinion, row six is the optimal spot. You're not so far up front as to be noticed by every single person who gets on the bus, but not so far back that the two stoner guys try to engage you in philosophical discussions about Fudgsicles.

The long morning bus ride is essential to my mental and psychological well-being. For one thing, Manneville High School is huge, collecting students from middle schools across the county, and it isn't hard to feel completely beside the point once you walk through its heavily alarmed front doors and merge into the hallway traffic. So it's important to have some time in the morning to remind yourself your life isn't totally insignificant, even if chances are slim you'll see anybody in the next seven hours who realizes it.

Monday bus rides are especially important. After a weekend of being around people who know my name, act as if what I say is reasonably interesting, and appreciate the contributions I make to the general welfare of the collective, it's a shock to find myself at school, where no one seems to have ever heard of me. Or if they have, it's because of that morning I spent walking around with a clump of straw in my hair until I ran into Sarah, who quickly plucked it out, or the week of the worm castings rash, or else the time—oh well, why dwell?

And you wonder why I eat lunch in the library.

"Today I'm going to eat in the cafeteria," I whisper into my notebook, the way I do every Monday, and then I slump down in my seat because I know I won't. If Sarah had B lunch, that would be one thing. Or if any of my old friends from Wheeler Middle, or just one single solitary person I recognized as a compadre, a sympathetic soul, a friendly face, a non-serial-killer type, were there to eat lunch with, I'd be fine. I'm not picky.

Unfortunately, B lunch is filled with football stars, prom queens, and ex-convicts, all of them total strangers and intimidating beyond belief. I lasted through two days of eating my egg salad sandwich and carrot sticks by myself, feeling small and exposed, like a fawn surrounded by hunters in pickup trucks with their headlights on high beam. I knew that no one was actually looking at me, and it soon became obvious that the only reason anyone would ever look at me was if I'd unwittingly come to school with, say, goat cheese smeared all over the back of my jeans. Feeling exposed and invisible at the same time was too much. I fled.

What made my loneliness even harder during those early days of my freshman year was my mother's assumption that I would love high school just as much as she had. She practically plowed me down the minute I got home to hear about my day. "High school is where it all begins, Janie," she'd enthused as she handed me a brownie and a glass of milk. "Now sit down and tell me everything that happened today."

My mumbled, unenthusiastic replies marked a change in our relationship. Up until my freshman year, I'd been happy to tell my mother the tiniest details of my day. I was famous among local mothers of middle school daughters for being the one who still confided in her mother, who still liked to go shopping with her mother, who still spoke in polysyllabic sentences to her mother. I'd read enough books and seen enough movies to recognize the weirdness of this for myself, but I honestly thought that things would never change between us. You know how some people never get acne? I thought I'd never get tired of my mother greeting me at the door every afternoon with milk and cookies.

I did.

In fact, it didn't take long before I could feel my chest tightening as I walked down the gravel driveway toward the house after the bus dropped me off. By the time I got through the door, I thought it was possible I might actually punch my mother if she said one more positive word to me about the wonders of freshman year. I started coming into the house through the screen porch so I could take the back staircase to my room and avoid her altogether.

Now, six weeks later, my mom no longer makes a big deal out of me being in high school. She has turned her energy and enthusiasm toward Avery, who loves the bejeebers out of third grade and the farm and doing stuff my mom loves to do, like baking and going to the flea market to buy hand-cranked grain mills and quilts so old that their original colors have faded into patches of gray and more gray. I lie on my bed upstairs and listen to them chirp together like birds, and I can't decide if what I'm feeling is sort of weirdly jealous or totally disdainful. It's a feeling that gets stuck in my throat, whatever it is.

The bus bounces over a series of potholes that bloomed last spring and are now enjoying the nice fall weather. The potholes mark ten more minutes until we reach Manneville High School, which means I have ten minutes to think cheerful, positive thoughts that will get me through the rest of my day. I remind myself that Sarah promised to leave a note in my locker before first period, a note that will be typed on an old manual typewriter that has become Sarah's trademark style, will run several single-spaced, hilarious pages, and will definitely include details from her older sister Emma's weekend escapades.

"We really ought to do Emma for our project," Sarah had said on Saturday, and I could see her point. Emma was not yet a historic figure, but undoubtedly would be one day, at least in the annals of Manneville High School. She's a straight-A student, honor roll every semester, and completely wild. No one has ever actually seen her crack a textbook, but pretty much everyone has seen her show up at school on the back of a Harley-Davidson, her hands wrapped around an authentic, very scary-looking biker named Todd, who works at the Harley shop in Rocky Mount and attends Renaissance fairs in his spare time, which is where Emma met him last fall.

It's the Renaissance fair detail that kills me. Emma is Harvard smart, cute, and has a sarcastic remark for every occasion. Girls like her don't do Renaissance fairs. But then Emma doesn't do anything girls like her are supposed to do. In fact, aside from making stellar grades, she mostly does the exact opposite.

Joking about choosing Emma as our project topic led us to come up with a list of bad girls of American history: Lizzie Borden, Bonnie of Bonnie and Clyde, Zelda Fitzgerald, Ma Barker, Madonna—

"And Emma Goldman," Sarah added, as though it were obvious. She likes to do that, throw out names of people or places that no one else has ever heard of and make it sound like common knowledge.

"Who's Emma Goldman?" I asked. I was years past pretending like I knew all of Sarah's little-known facts and figures when I actually didn't. I'd been burned too many times acting like I was as well informed as Sarah-pedia.

Sarah leaned back in her seat, an old-fashioned heavy desk chair on wheels. "Emma Goldman was your basic proto-feminist, radical socialist freethinker. She's who Emma was named after."

"Your parents named Emma after a radical socialist freethinker?"

"Well, actually, my parents named Emma after my grandmother," Sarah admitted. "My grandmother was the one who was named after Emma Goldman."

"So how'd your dad end up such a total Republican?"

Sarah grimaced. "Bad seed. Every family's got one."

We discussed the possibility of doing our project on Emma Goldman, but Sarah was afraid it might get her grounded. Her parents were well aware of Emma Goldman's thoughts on free love, and it could be safely assumed the Lymans didn't share them. So that left us . . . nowhere.

"But all kidding aside," I said after a few minutes of both of us looking glumly around the room as if our project topic would suddenly pop out of Sarah's overstuffed closet along with her tennis racket and the purple platform sandals she'd found last summer at One More Time, our favorite thrift shop. "Wouldn't it be cool if we actually could do Emma? I mean Emma, your sister."

Sarah nodded. "Or at least someone who's interesting, but not everybody knows about. Somebody who has a story that needs to be told, somebody whose story has been kept a secret for a long time—"

Sarah was starting to ramp up the rhetoric, which had been happening with alarming frequency since her decision to enter international politics. I quickly cut her off. "Yeah, maybe someone local. Like that woman who started the community garden over near the homeless shelter."

"Yeah, okay, maybe," Sarah said in a super-supportive tone that meant no way was she doing the community gardening lady, but she was willing to humor me until she figured something else out. "Well, this is a good start. Why don't we each come up with a list and go over it on Monday in class, discuss the pros and cons of our ideas, and see what's going to work best in the long run?"

Sarah lives and dies by the pro/con list. Every major

decision she's made in her life—whether to play flute or trumpet in band, whether to accept Clark Merritt's invitation to the eighth-grade dance, whether to buy a bikini or a one-piece—has been made by considering the pros (flutes are lighter and involve less spit) and the cons (going to the dance with Clark Merritt could quite possibly mark her as a dweeb forever) of a situation. Once the pros and cons are added and subtracted and a decision is reached, Sarah never looks back.

The bus passes what I've come to think of as the "one mile away from school, and it's time to panic" mark—an oak tree split in half by lightning that I swear looks like an old man standing with his arms wide open like he's asking, "What? What did I do that was so wrong?" I open my notebook and look over my uninspired list. Community garden lady. Jennifer Phillips, a reporter my mom used to work with, who uncovered a major nursing-home scandal three years ago and won a ton of journalism prizes for it. Marie Murray, a professor in my dad's department who teaches blind kids to play violin.

I lean my head back and close my eyes, which is what I usually do when we hit the dreaded one-mile mark. By this time, the bus has filled up with competing scents—serious applications of spicy aftershaves and citrusy body mists, the minty smell of toothpaste, wintergreen gum, Altoids, the slight whiff of a recently smoked joint, and the unfortunate odor of gym shoes long past their prime, all mixed up with lung-crushing exhaust fumes (but thankfully no goat poop)—and I feel sort of sick, a feeling that will most likely stay with me for the rest of the day.

I wish I could come up with a great project topic, if only to impress the twelve girls and one guy who take Great Girls and Women of American History. Just once this year, I want someone to look at me and think, *Huh, she seems kind of neat* instead of *Huh, I wonder why she smells like manure.* Just once I want someone to think, *What a nice, normal human being with totally good ideas.* Just one single time I want someone to think, *Hey, that Janie Gorman's pretty interesting.*

Because I am, you know. And not just because I talk to goats.

Chapter Five

Lemmingville

As promised, Sarah's note is waiting for me, taped to the inside of my locker door. The morning note is a long tradition between us, established after my family moved to Farm World. We talk on the phone all the time and text each other constantly, but that's not enough somehow. Besides, in this age of technological wonders, actually writing words on paper using your own hand and that crude device known as an ink pen (or in Sarah's case, a manual typewriter) seems really cool and countercultural.

We got that idea from Emma, of course. We get all of our cool, countercultural ideas from her.

Dear Janiesayqua, the note begins, and continues, *Janie say wha—? Please get it through your head that this is going to be a most fantabulous day.*

Typical Sarah. She's disturbed that I'm still eating lunch in the library after two months of high school. She thinks

I should be past that by now. This is easy for Miss A lunch to say, she who has spent every lunch period since the first day of school surrounded by our old friends from Wheeler Middle, she who has algebra with Lauren Basco and Sonia Meeker, English I with Rebecca Wade and Hannah Anders, and PE with all of the above plus Marcy Wilder, Wren Briggs, and Hannah Wolfe.

Please eat lunch in the cafeteria today! (See, what did I tell you?) *There's a really cool girl in PE named MacKenzie who has B lunch. She went to McDougal for middle school, but she isn't scary at all, and she has a lot of friends who did Battle of the Books last year, so you know they're our kind of people.*

I fold Sarah's note and put it in the front pocket of my backpack. I like to stretch it out over the course of the morning, saving a big chunk of it for lunch, the social nadir of my day.

The halls are not just crowded. They are not merely packed. They are overrun, like termite-infested logs. That anyone can actually move at all is a miracle of modern physics. Manneville High School is famous for the state of its bursting seams. New subdivisions pop up on the outskirts of town on a daily basis, feeding more and more lemmings into the stream of public education, and yet no one can quite work up the interest to build a new high school.

I've volunteered to quit, just to make more room, on

several occasions since the beginning of school, but my parents think I'm joking.

I'm not.

I duck my head and begin the seemingly uphill climb to Algebra I with Mrs. Gina Redfearn, the oldest teacher in captivity, and maybe the meanest. "I'm old school, people," she warned us the first day of class. "I'm not here to make friends." And she's really not, as she made abundantly clear on Day One, when she gave us a pop quiz immediately after calling roll. The first day. And it *counted.*

I've found the secret to surviving Algebra I with Mrs. Redfearn is to keep your head down. Literally. She takes direct eye contact as an act of aggression and responds in kind. There are just enough do-gooder straight-A types in this class, kids who are all about direct eye contact and class participation, to keep Mrs. Redfearn occupied through the entire forty-three-minute period.

Today, first thing, there's a quiz on graphing linear equations, which makes perfect sense, since we haven't actually begun our unit on linear equations. After I turn in my paper, an inventive little number that's sure to earn me a juicy red zero, I return to my seat and train my eyes on my Algebra I notebook, thus rendering myself invisible for the rest of the period.

There are other kids in the class who have figured out this trick, though some make the mistake of falling asleep, which doesn't go unnoticed by Mrs. R. Among those of us who manage to keep our eyelids propped open, there are a fair number of doodlers, a handful of thorough note takers, two math geniuses who get started on their homework for the following day, not needing any of Mrs. Redfearn's algebraic insights to help them along, and the occasional outlaw text messager. I'm an in-betweener, taking notes for as long as I can stand it, then falling into doodleland.

Today I start doodling Mrs. Redfearn, wondering, as I have many times before, about Mr. Redfearn, what his life must be like, or if in fact there is a Mr. Redfearn at all. I doodle a picture of an old man who comes out looking like Mr. Pritchard. It's impossible to imagine Mrs. Redfearn married to someone like Mr. Pritchard, though. Mr. Pritchard, while eighty-nine and imprisoned in a nursing home, still embraces life and all its wonders. Mrs. Redfearn is an anti-life force if I ever saw one.

I draw Mrs. Redfearn standing next to Mr. Pritchard, then quickly turn her into a tree. I cannot, even in a doodle, subject Mr. Pritchard to my algebra teacher. I like him too much.

"He's a pretty good old boy, isn't he?" my father remarked on our way home Saturday. He has this way of talking after we've visited with Mr. Pritchard that reminds you he grew up in Rome, Georgia, that my dad is, in fact, a redneck for peace. At other times, while you'd never mistake my dad for, say, a native New Yorker, his southern roots sort of hide under his tweed jacket and professor's briefcase.

I nodded, although "pretty good old boy" doesn't do Mr. Pritchard justice. He was a civil rights lawyer back in the 1950s and '60s, and even had a cross burned on his front lawn. "Me and the wife, we just got out the marshmallows and roasted them over the flames," he told us during our first session. "Went back inside when they started shooting at us, of course."

My dad wasn't actually interviewing Mr. Pritchard about his involvement in the civil rights movement. He was interviewing Mr. Pritchard about his yard art (Mr. Pritchard had left the cross on the lawn and used it as a trellis for morning glories). My dad teaches in the folklore department at the university and is always doing oral history projects on obscure but strangely fascinating topics, like snake handlers and barbecue pit masters and fast-track go-cart racers.

The first time we went to see Mr. Pritchard was six months ago when he still lived in his own house. My dad had asked me to come along to help him set up his recording equipment and monitor sound levels. I'd been helping him out since I was eleven, lugging in mic stands and sound monitors from the back of my dad's truck like a roadie, standing by silently while my dad talked to people—in this case, most of them elderly, yard art being a dying art—about their tire planters and washing machine doghouses, their venom tolerance and theories about chopped pork versus pulled. Sometimes it was boring, but I always tried to look interested as a professional courtesy.

But Mr. Pritchard was anything but boring. He'd start telling my dad about the bluebird houses he'd built for his backyard, and before you knew it he was describing the death threats he'd gotten during particularly contentious cases. "Old Ellis Watkins called me up trying to disguise his voice, said he was going to chop me up and feed me to his hogs for supper."

When we went to see him at the nursing home on Saturday, Mr. Pritchard was napping in a chair beside his bed. My dad tapped him on the shoulder and said, "Harlan?" and Mr. Pritchard startled awake. "Hazel?" he mumbled, looking around for his wife, who's been dead for five years. He shook his head, noticed my dad, and said, "Oh, Mike, it's you. How you doing, son?"

My dad gripped Mr. Pritchard's shoulder in a kind of guy mini-hug. "You're looking good, Harlan. How the ladies treating you?"

Mr. Pritchard calls all the female nurses and aides at the nursing home "the ladies."

"They can't resist me, Mike," Mr. Pritchard told him, pushing himself up from his chair, which he offered to me. I shook my head, nodding toward the two boxes of equipment, which I began to set up. "Got to beat 'em off with a stick."

Mr. Pritchard walked over to his bed and boosted himself up. His legs dangled over the side like a little kid's. "My voice isn't feeling all that strong today, Mike. You want to sit next to me on the bed while we talk?"

I set up the mic stand in front of Mr. Pritchard and positioned the microphone so it was angled toward his mouth. Pulling the monitor over to the chair next to the sink, I sat down and began adjusting the sound levels, feeling competent and tech savvy as I twisted and turned the knobs, although this is the only technical expertise I actually possess, and only because I've been helping my dad with his interviews for years now.

After my father announced into the mic the date and place of the interview, and that the interview was with Harlan Pritchard of Manneville, North Carolina, he began with his questions. "Now, Harlan, last time we were discussing the medicinal herbs that Hazel grew for teas on the east side of the house. Tell me some of the names, if you would, and how Hazel propagated plants, that sort of thing."

Mr. Pritchard shifted forward toward the mic. "Well, sir, Hazel was a seed collector. If you had a plant she found interesting, she wouldn't waste any time asking you to fill her an envelope up with some seeds."

After an hour, Mr. Pritchard's voice began to grow raspy, and it was easy to see he was getting tired. "I'm not much good to you today, Mike," he said finally. "Couldn't sleep at all last night. Some old girl down the hall was crying for her babies. Saddest thing you ever heard. I'm glad my Hazel never had to go through this"—he waved his arm around the room, pointing at the heart monitor next his bed and the bedpan on his bedside table. "Terrible way to finish things up."

I can't stop thinking about Mr. Pritchard, the way he stays so cheerful even with the bedpans and the crying, and by the time the bell rings to release us from first period, my doodling has grown into a full-fledged portrait. He's standing in the middle of his front yard surrounded by birdhouses filled with bluebirds. Mrs. Pritchard, who Mr. Pritchard has talked about so much I feel like I know her, peeks around from the corner of the house, a bouquet of flowers in her hands. I've seen her picture, so I know to make her eyes all crinkly. She ends up looking like Emma.

I tear out the page from my notebook and put it in my backpack, next to Sarah's note. As I stand and scoop up my books, I remember something Mr. Pritchard told me about Hazel—she was a teacher. She wasn't a public school teacher, though. She taught people how to read and write so that they could register to vote.

"Got a window shot out for that," Mr. Pritchard recalled

when he told my dad about it. "Got shot at too. But Hazel wasn't afraid. Only thing that ever made her afraid was that the bad guys might win in the end."

Hazel Pritchard. I grab my notebook out of my back-pack and scribble her name under Marie Murray's. Then I duck my head and shoulder my way toward world history, occasionally glancing up to see if anyone's interested in making eye contact in a welcoming, "maybe we could be friends" sort of way.

Guess what?

They aren't.

Chapter Six

Lunch Bunch

Let me just clarify one thing: I don't actually eat lunch in the library. Food and beverages are not allowed, as the signage posted every two feet will tell you. So I scarf down my lunch standing in front of my locker, then head for sanctuary.

The first thing I do when I get there is find an open computer and check out my mom's blog. Each new post is an adventure in potential humiliation, but somehow I can't help myself. I have to see how my mom has reconstructed her homemade life for public viewing.

My mom is a freelance journalist, which is to say a writer who doesn't make any money. She used to be a reporter at the *Manneville Gazette,* but when Avery was born she downgraded to correspondent, which meant she contributed the occasional article, but most nights fell asleep in front of the computer, too tired to type. After we moved out to Farm World, she quit the paper entirely and began working on a memoir about—wait for it—moving out to Farm World. Step one for writing a memoir: blogging a memoir.

"I want to respect your privacy," she told me a few days before she launched Gone Country (subtitle: Notes on a Homemade Life). "I won't post any pictures of you, but there might be times I want to write about you or use something you've said. Is that okay?"

Was it okay? I was ten and a half. My mother was going to make me famous! It was more than okay. It was excellent!

And for a little while, it really was. In my mother's portraits of mini-farm life—the day the goats arrived, her misadventures in beekeeping, how she finally learned to bake bread—I came off as a bright, philosophical kid who had interesting insights into the inner lives of chickens. Avery was the mischievous little girl always getting into scrapes. My dad, who my mom always refers to as DH for Darling Husband, was portrayed as a "let's look on the bright side of things" kind of guy, the pillar my ever-bumbling mother (this is how she presents herself in her blog—the woman who messes stuff up in charming, amusing ways, misreads instructions, puts in an order for fifty pounds of marigold seed when she meant to ask for five packets) leans on in times of distress.

When did it begin to go sour for me? Was it the time she veered ever so slightly off the topic of mini-farm life to report on my first boy-girl party, when I was eleven and a half? She pretended the party at Quaid Porter's house had something to do with life on the farm because it happened to be on the day Patsy Cline had her first litter (and yes, she made connections between goat babies and spin the bottle, much to my alarm), but the fact is, she was just looking for an excuse to talk about the fact that I was growing up.

Admittedly, for the most part my mom sticks to Farm World in her posts. The problem is, since she started Gone Country three years ago, it's become sort of a local institution. The *Manneville Gazette* ran a feature on my mom and her blog a year or so after she'd started blogging, and suddenly everyone seemed to be reading it. My mom went from getting three or four comments per post to chalking up twenty-five to thirty. People around town with their own mini-farm dreams started living vicariously through her. The library asked her to give a lecture series on living sustainably on five acres or less. A group inspired by my mother's chicken musings began a movement to overturn a long-standing ordinance against keeping chickens within city limits. My mom was asked to give a speech to the city council, and many of her fans credit her passionate oration with making chickens legal in Manneville proper.

So people far and wide have a thrice-weekly window into my family's life, and while my guess is that aside from my close friends none of my peers (a) are aware that my mother and her blog exist, and (b) wouldn't read my mother's blog if they were aware of it, nevertheless it's nervous-making to know that at any given time people who might possibly be persuaded to know and love me could read three years' worth of archives about my family and our life down on the farm.

I look around the library as I'm waiting for my mom's page to load. It's the usual B lunch suspects, the tall kid with his question mark slouch and purple acne reading steadily through back issues of *Nintendo Power* at the round table by the radiator, the two guys who appear to be on the lam from sixth grade working a Rubik's cube as they sit next to each other on matching orange beanbag chairs, passing the puzzle back and forth and muttering frustrated obscenities. A round girl with angelic yellow curls writes with a Sharpie pen in a thick, hardback journal, occasionally stopping to doodle another black ink tattoo on her left arm.

Once in a while someone appears who gives you hope, a cute boy reading the latest *Sports Illustrated* or a girl of the normal-looking variety thumbing through the books on the "This Just In!" cart. Are they cafeteria refugees too? But they never show up two days in a row, and my hopes for finding friendship in the library are dashed yet again.

That's my dream, of course. That some regular, everyday people will show up and recognize me as someone who is basically normal, in spite of my Farm Girl mishaps, but whose soul is too sensitive to deal with the cafeteria alone. We will become friends and find other B lunch refugees, hiding out in the back of the school auditorium or hovering around the edges of the newspaper office, pretending to have a lead on a big story. When we've banded together enough troops, we'll take over a table in the cafeteria and never be lonely again.

Looking around, I see that once again I'm out of luck. I turn back to the computer screen, and there's the picture of the chickenmobile directly over the banner that asks in bright yellow letters whether or not I'm ready for the country. *Sure, why not,* I think, and click on the downward cursor.

Today my mom has blogged about the trip she and Avery took Saturday to the flea market over at the state fair grounds. In the last two years, my mother has become a huge fan of getting as much of your stuff secondhand as possible. Not just clothes and books, but tools, linens, and small kitchen appliances. Saturday she and Avery found a treadle sewing machine. They spent most of Sunday cleaning and oiling it, then giving it about a hundred test runs before they got a straight seam. It's actually a pretty cool machine. Too bad my mom can't sew.

She admits as much at the beginning of paragraph two in today's post. *I can't tell you how much I now regret rejecting my mother's offers to teach me to sew when I was young,* she writes. *She'll smile when she hears I got this machine.*

My grandmother will fall out of her chair laughing when she hears my mom got a sewing machine. Everything my mother does these days cracks Grammy up. As a teenager, my mother swore she would never stay at home to raise children, she would never learn to cook, and she would never submit herself to the tyranny of yard work—she'd pave her yard over if she ever had one.

And now here she is, with her very own mini-farm and a sewing machine.

I've decided to make as many of our clothes as possible from now on, my mom suddenly declares at the beginning of paragraph four, and I actually choke on my own saliva. I sputter and turn red-faced. Mrs. Welsch, the librarian, looks at me in alarm, but I wave her off. A little spittle in the old windpipe won't kill anybody.

On the other hand, having to wear clothes sewn by my mom just might.

You have to understand about my mom. She's very competent as a rule, and highly intelligent. When she puts her mind to something—like learning to cook or starting a blog, for instance—she's determined and ultimately successful.

Except when it comes to arts and crafts.

My mother has tried knitting, crocheting, and cross-stitch. She has taken up pottery, basket making, and weaving. She has failed miserably in each attempt. It's a sad cycle to witness, actually. You know something's about to start when she comes home with a gleam in her eye and a shopping bag from Michael's or A.C. Moore. "From now on we're making our own Christmas cards," is the sort of thing she'll declare, dumping a bundle of rubber stamps and ink pads onto the kitchen table.

Now, who could mess up rubber stamping? you're probably wondering, and the answer is: my mom. Her stamped images turn out blurry, the ink gets all over her hands and her clothes, and by the end of her efforts to make our Christmas cards, she's in such a fluster my dad has to buy her dinner and a bottle of wine just to get her calmed down again.

When it comes to creative endeavors, my mom should stick to perfecting her basil-cremini pizza sauce.

I log off the computer and, feeling a little shaky, take a seat at my usual table, two tables over from Angel Hair Tattoo Girl. Visions of me dressed in homemade clothes dance like sugarplums-gone-bad in my head. I see the sagging hemlines, the left sleeves shorter than the right sleeves, the fabric bunching up in all sorts of unfortunate places. What if my mom decides to make jeans? Can you make jeans at home?

Oh. Please. No.

"Are you okay?" Angel Hair Tattoo Girl whispers across the tables, and I realize I've been whimpering. I nod, and she takes my nod as an invitation to move closer.

"You seem a little freaked out," she tells me in a slightly louder voice as she takes the seat beside me. "Which, believe me, I know all about. Every day of my life is a freak-out day."

I look at her Sharpie tattoos and believe her.

"Like today?" she continues, apparently needing no encouragement from me to go on. "I wake up and there's, like, totally nothing to wear. My mom's in Europe on this business trip. And my dad is useless. You know, like, welcome to the twenty-first century, Dad, where men do laundry, right?"

I nod. Right. *Kids, too,* I think, but keep it to myself.

"So what choice do I have except raid my mom's closet, which she would kill me for if she knew. But here's the weird part." She pauses for dramatic effect, and I check out her outfit, which is nice, but unremarkable, a soft black sweater and a dark brown velour skirt over black tights and very cool-looking biker boots. "What's really weird is my mom's clothes smell like her. I mean, her perfume, and so all day it's like my mom has been walking right beside me. Which, you have to admit, is a pretty freaky feeling."

"That would be pretty freaky," I agree.

"Hey, did you ever read that book, *Freaky Friday*? Where the mom and the daughter change places?"

And she's off again. All I have to do to encourage her to keep talking is to nod and smile at the right places. I don't even have to listen to what she's saying. I can tell by the rise and fall of her voice, the dramatic pauses, and the "You know what I mean's" when it's time to rejoin the conversation.

Occasionally I take a moment to look around the library in hopes that someone is witnessing Janie Gorman personally and positively interacting with another human being.

Sadly, no one is.

The bell rings. Angel Hair Tattoo Girl stands. She smiles at me and extends her hand. "I'm Verbena. It's nice to meet you. I see you here all the time."

I take her hand, shake it. Her grip is surprisingly firm. I can't help but ask, "Verbena?"

She shrugs. "Yeah, I know." She bobs her head side to side in the international sign for *I'm a goofball, what can I say?* "My mom thought it sounded French. But you know what? After I started taking French, I realized it doesn't sound French at all. It sounds like the name of some rundown eastern European country."

I laugh. Mrs. Welsch, who completely ignored Verbena's twenty-minute monologue, gives me the evil eye and the "shush" signal, index finger to pouty lips, but I don't care. There's something about Verbena that I like. Maybe it's that for the last twenty minutes she's taken my mind off the outfits my mom plans to make for me just as soon as she learns to thread a needle without drawing blood.

"I'll see you here tomorrow, okay?" Verbena asks over her shoulder, retrieving her journal and Sharpie from her table. "It was really cool talking to you."

I wave and gather my books. I try not to think about Verbena's Sharpie tattoos. When the hand of friendship is offered, it's bad manners to refuse it, even if it's covered with tiny black peace signs and roses and—what were those other things, anyway? Angels of Death?

Doesn't matter. Somebody talked to me. Verbena the Tattooed Girl talked to me.

I have arrived.

Chapter Seven

In Which Life Imitates Robert Rauschenberg

I don't have any friends in Art I, but as a place I have to be every day, it's not so bad. Not as good as Great Girls and Women, because Sarah's not in it, but better than just about anything else. For one thing, the teacher, Ms. Ashdown, is both humane and reasonable. She's funny, she's cool, but she actually expects you to work in class and turn in your projects on time. On the respect-o-meter, Ms. Ashdown gets high marks. Add to that, she's praised my "color instinct" three times this semester.

I'm a fan.

I thought art was where I'd make friends, and some possibilities exist, but nothing has panned out yet. There's a quiet, pale girl named Meg who sits off by herself, sketches constantly, and has a tendency toward interesting socks. When we have group critiques, she's the one everyone listens to. She can be critical, but she's never unkind, and she's always right. The problem is, other than group critique, she doesn't talk. I complimented her once on a drawing, and she smiled very nicely and sort of nodded. Then she went right back to sketching without a word. She's refused to make eye contact with me ever since.

I take my seat at the table between Chester and Lynnette. They are a friendly, chatty, and outgoing duo. Unfortunately, they are, in fact, a duo, so I spend much of my time in art leaning way forward or way back so they can barrage each other with love taps and deep, meaningful looks. If they had reason to believe that anybody besides themselves existed in Art I, I'm sure we'd be the best of friends. Who knows, maybe they'll break up, and not only will I have two new friends, I'll be able to undo the damage to my spinal cord caused by being made to sit between the two of them.

As Ms. Ashdown goes over the roll, I sneak a peek at Sarah's note. She's moved past who I should sit with at lunch to her latest update on the Chocolate Wars. For a fund-raiser, the third graders in her neighborhood, students at Sewall Elementary, are selling chocolate made from Ivory Coast cocoa beans. Sarah has composed a letter to the school's principal and PTA president explaining to them why they should sell fair trade chocolate instead. She will, she promises, e-mail me a copy for proofreading.

"Okay, my young friends, today we're talking Rauschenberg!" Ms. Ashdown calls out. The classroom lights dim and the PowerPoint presentation begins. "Robert Rauschenberg was famous for saying he wanted to work in the gap between art and life," Ms. Ashdown tells us. "He believed that everyday, ordinary things could be art."

We spend a lot of the class period looking at Rauschenberg's collages. We see stuffed birds and Coca-Cola bottles, bits of newspaper and fabric, photographs, tires, doors, and windows, all assembled on huge canvases. Somebody mutters, "I don't get it," and Ms. Ashdown replies, "Whose fault is that? Yours or the artist's? I'm willing to entertain either answer, but I want you to actually think before you speak."

That shuts the mutterer right up. And keeps me from raising my hand and saying that I don't get it either. How is a tire stuck on a canvas art? What's beautiful about a stick or a torn piece of newspaper? I'm not an art Neanderthal—we've spent the last four weeks on the abstract expressionists and I loved them, especially the ones who weren't afraid to throw a little color out there—but I don't know what to think about art that looks like it got pulled from a recycling bin.

So when Ms. Ashdown informs us that, yes, big surprise, we're starting a unit on collage, I groan a little on the inside. Because I know she's going to expect us to come up with junkyard projects, Rauschenberg-esque projects. I'm already nostalgic for the days spent in art class splashing paint on the canvas à la Jackson Pollock, fun, frolicsome days, days you could feel creative without going through the Dumpster to collect your materials.

To add insult to injury, two seconds later Chester accidently smacks me in the back of the head as he's reaching his hand toward Lynnette.

"Wow, man, I'm so sorry," he yelps, and begins rubbing my head where he's smacked it. "Total accident."

Lynnette glares at him. "Quit rubbing her head, moron! She doesn't want you touching her!"

"It's okay," I assure both of them. "Just a little strange. I mean—"

But neither of them is paying attention to me anymore. They've already fallen back into Chester 'n' Lynnette world, apologizing and making lovey-dovey cooing noises at each other.

I glance up at the clock. Three minutes left of class. Not enough time to start stapling shoelaces to a piece of poster board, but plenty of time to finish reading Sarah's note so that I'll be fully briefed by the time I see her.

The funny thing is, when I start to read I can't help but imagining Robert Rauschenberg cutting out words from Sarah's typewritten pages for a collage: *chocolate, elementary, sweet, biodegradable, love.*

I suppose I wouldn't mind making a collage that had

a few words in it. Sure, it's not the same as mounting a stuffed Angora goat's head on a piece of canvas (which, yes, Robert Rauschenberg did, thank you very much), but at least I won't be getting any angry phone calls from PETA. I'll take words over a goat's head any day.

Which is why I carry the note over to the self-healing mat at the back of the room and use an X-Acto knife to cut each word out in a precise, tiny rectangle. I ask Ms. Ashdown for an envelope and deposit the words inside.

Then I take the picture I drew in algebra of Mr. and Mrs. Pritchard and put that in the envelope too, and I put the envelope in the front pocket of my backpack.

It's not a collage exactly, but at least it's something I can live with.

Chapter Eight

It's for a Good Cause

By the time I get to Great Girls and Women of American History, my last class of the day, I've made it all the way through Sarah's note. I learn what the Lymans had for dinner Saturday night (extra-large take-out meat-busters pizza) and how Sarah got out of going to church Sunday morning (claimed to have cramps—total lie), which is her goal every week. She hates to miss the political talk shows, just in case someone mentions cocoa beans.

And then comes the shocking news: Emma has been grounded for curfew violations. I had no idea Emma even had a curfew. I always assumed that as long as she kept her grades up and stayed away from the long arm of the law, she was free to do as she pleased. Besides, people like Emma don't get grounded. They get sent to the guillotine or military school. Getting grounded is what happens to normal people.

Todd dropped Emma off at three a.m., Sarah had written in her note. *His Harley woke up the whole neighborhood. You should have heard my dad when he got outside. It was like an opera out there—Emma shrieking at my dad, my dad yelling at the top of his lungs, Todd revving his engine, all the neighborhood dogs barking. That's got to be a violation of the neighborhood covenant. (Does Shady Woods have a covenant? And if so, is it constitutional? I'll have to check.)*

Sarah is sitting in a lounge chair at the back of the classroom when I get there. In Ms. Morrison's classroom the desks are pulled together in a tight circle with a round, bright orange rug in the middle, and the corners are filled with various beach chairs and loungers for when her classes break into groups. Ms. Morrison is the sort of teacher who can't go ten minutes without breaking her class into groups, which is why nothing ever gets done during class time. Ninety-five percent of the work done for Great Girls and Woman of American History is strictly extracurricular.

Sarah holds up her notebook when she sees me, and even from across the room I can see the pro/con line dividing the page into two neat columns.

"I think we've got to go with Geraldine," she tells me when I pull up a wobbly chaise lounge beside her. "Her pros outweigh anybody else's on our list."

"*Au contraire,* Pierre," I say. "I think I've got an idea

you're going to like even more than Geraldine."

The bell rings, and Ms. Morrison breezes into the classroom, papers spilling out of her organizer, a sticky note stuck to her elbow. "Continue on, everyone!" she says. "Project ideas due at the end of class!"

Since no one actually stopped talking when she entered the room, continuing on is not a problem. In fact, two months into the school year, our small class treats Ms. Morrison as an afterthought. Even when we're gathered together as a group, Ms. Morrison is rarely the center of attention. That honor goes to Marley Baxter, a radical feminist sophomore who on the first day of class wanted to hold a vote on whether or not the class's lone boy, Wallace, should be allowed to stay. Sarah campaigned vigorously on Wallace's behalf and he was voted in, 11–2, but Marley continued to behave as if the class were hers to lead, and after a while, the rest of us generally accepted her command. For one thing, she's pretty free with the bathroom passes.

I pull my list from my notebook and hand it to Sarah, who quickly eyeballs it and shrugs. "It looks great and everything, except that I don't actually know who these women are, and if I don't know, then it goes without saying . . ."

She waves her arm vaguely around, which I'm supposed to interpret to mean that if Sarah doesn't know, nobody knows.

I take my list back and point to Hazel Pritchard's name. "Mrs. Pritchard was very involved in the civil rights movement." I pause, then say in a singsongy voice, "You know how much you like civil rights stuff."

Civil rights is the one political issue the whole Lyman family can agree upon. Civil rights for all Americans = Good. And last year Emma got completely wrapped up in it. She'd read this book called *Blood Done Sign My Name* by Timothy B. Tyson, about the murder of a black man by a white man and the subsequent trial back in the 1970s, thirty miles north of here. She took a road trip to the town where the murder happened and wrote a forty-page paper about it, which her teacher wanted her to try to publish in an academic journal.

This gives me an idea. "What if we got Emma to help us? She might, right? Okay, probably not, but maybe. I mean, I know it's a long shot and everything. . . ."

Sarah's eyes widen. An Emma opportunity! Have I mentioned that both of us worship Emma as the Queen of Cool? Rest assured that the feeling is not mutual. It's not that Emma's rude or actively unkind; she just doesn't seem to realize that either Sarah or I exist in any sort of meaningful way. If we were pets, we'd be goldfish; if we were a sport, we'd be Ping-Pong. No, we'd be a Ping-Pong table covered with folded laundry.

I watch Sarah working out the possibilities of my

suggestion in her head. A civil rights project is right up Emma's alley. You can even imagine Emma feeling a little jealous that it's not her project. You can even imagine Emma looking up to us for coming up with such an amazing plan.

Okay, so you can't really imagine Emma looking up to us. Neither can we. In fact, Sarah shakes her head a little, as if that little bit of fantasy has just occurred to her and she's trying to dislodge it from her brain.

"All right," she says after another minute. "The Mrs. Pritchard project has definite potential, I have to admit."

"It really does," I agree cheerfully.

"I bet there are old newspaper articles we could find." Sarah plucks a pen from behind her ear and begins to fill up a new page of her notebook. "We'll need to do interviews. Emma can take us."

She says this matter-of-factly, as if Emma was always giving us a ride somewhere. Emma has never given us a ride anywhere, of course, even though she's had her driver's license for a year and a half. She has exactly the sort of car you'd want to be seen in too—a beat-up baby blue Volkswagen Beetle with cool political bumper stickers plastered across the back. Now I imagine myself in the backseat, the wind blowing through my hair as we drive off in pursuit of truth and justice and the American way.

It probably won't ever happen, but a girl can dream.

We spend the rest of the period working out the fine points of our project. At five minutes before the bell, Marley Baxter yells out, "All right, folks, I'll be coming around to pick up your project proposals, so have 'em ready." Sarah writes our names neatly across the top of our paper, then nods approvingly at our work.

"This is important," she declares. "From everything you've told me, Hazel Pritchard was a hero. People should know about her."

"I bet doing research on Mrs. Pritchard will be a lot more fun than on Geraldine Ferraro," I add.

Sarah looks at me as if to ask, *Geraldine who?*

And then she looks at her watch and grins. "Hey, hey, it's Jeremy Fitch time."

We lean toward each other and slap high fives.

Jeremy Fitch time is the highlight of our day.

Chapter Nine

Jeremy Fitch: An Overview

Jeremy Fitch came into our lives two months ago, the first day of freshman year. Sarah and I were rounded up with the rest of the ninth graders and herded into the auditorium, where we sat through a gamut of speeches from administrators about rules and more rules and the terrible things that would happen to us if we violated a single one of them. Following that, we heard a speech about school spirit from the captain of the football team and the head varsity cheerleader, the gist of which was, if you don't have school spirit, forget about getting into the college of your choice.

I was wriggling in my seat, so eager was I to be filled with the spirit of Manneville High. I wanted to raise my hand and sign up for something—anything! everything!—right away. This was three days before the haystack-in-my-hair incident, three days before I'd walk cluelessly from class to class wondering why people were pointing at the back of my head and guffawing, three days before I'd stomp up the stairs to my room the minute I got home, yelling at my mom that I didn't want to talk about high school ever again so she could just shut up about it right that very second.

The student body president, Megan Vanderbilt, came onstage to tell us how to Get Active. "There's so much to do at Manneville High!" she exclaimed, and immediately I wanted to be student body president. I wanted to be Megan Vanderbilt, shiny and clean and pretty and *involved*.

Over the course of fifteen minutes, Megan brought out representatives of various clubs and let them do their thing. The Drama Club kids performed a two-minute skit, the debaters debated heatedly for ninety seconds. The last group to come up was the Manneville High School Jam Band. "These guys get together on Friday afternoons in the band room and just jam!" Megan said, sounding giddy and amazed. "And everybody's welcome!"

And then, there he was, though we didn't know his name yet. Jeremy Fitch, tall and lanky, his dark hair falling over his eyes as he strummed an electric guitar. He was wearing a gray Durham Bulls T-shirt under an unbuttoned blue flannel shirt, khaki cargo shorts, and low-top black Chucks, no socks. When he glanced up at the audience, his clear blue eyes seemed to look straight at me and

Sarah, and he grinned for a second before bending over his guitar again.

Sarah elbowed me excitedly. "He was looking straight at us! What do you think that means?"

"He's in love," I replied. "But how ever can he choose between us?"

Sarah elbowed me again, but this time it hurt. "I'm serious. He really did smile at us."

"They say sometimes when babies smile, it's actually gas," I said, refusing to take seriously that the cute boy onstage had singled me and Sarah out of the crowd. High school was shaping up to be the best time of my life, what with pep rallies and team spirit and all those wonderful, myriad ways to be involved, but there was no way it could be *that* good. But a few seconds later, it happened again. He raised his head, looked our way, and smiled a crooked smile that made me feel lightheaded.

"See? You saw that, right?" Sarah gripped my arm. "That look was definitely *not* a figment of my imagination."

After the assembly ended, instead of heading directly to first period, Sarah and I took a right down hallway B and found the auditorium's side door. We tried to look casual, like this was where we always hung out after school assemblies, just a couple of awesome babes chillin'. A few minutes later the members of the Jam Band straggled out, and there he was, whatever his name was, the cute guitar player of our dreams.

"That was great," Sarah said to the cute guitar player as he passed us. "You sounded so good up there."

The boy stopped, looked around at the other guys with his eyebrows raised, then turned back to Sarah. "Thanks," he told her. "Do you play?"

"I've always wanted to play guitar," she lied. "How good do you have to be to jam with you guys?"

"A lot of us really stink," the boy said, laughing. "So you don't have to be good at all. Too bad you don't play bass, though. We could use a bass player."

"Maybe I'll try it," Sarah said with a casual toss of her hair. "My name is Sarah Lyman, by the way."

I stared at her, impressed by how cool she was acting. Sarah had always been better at talking to guys than I was, although she did have a tendency to lecture about the Clean Air Act and how we all needed to come to the aid of famine victims. Still, this exchange today, complete with casual hair tosses, was a new high.

A guy who'd been tapping a pair of drumsticks against a locker in a bored sort of way asked, "You related to Emma Lyman?"

Sarah nodded proudly. The cute guitar player guy grinned at her like he was seeing her for the first time.

"Awesome," the drummer replied, and a couple of the other guys nodded.

Sarah put her hand on my shoulder to draw me into the conversation. "And this is my best friend, Janie. Janie Gorman. She's a great singer."

I glared at Sarah. I like to sing, but by no definition of the word am I a great or even very good singer. My talent is for singing along with CDs and songs on the radio. As long as another voice is coming out of a nearby speaker, I can hit a tune note for note. Turn the stereo off, my singing is toast. Not that I would admit that to the cute boy standing in front of me.

"I'm Jeremy," the cute guitar player guy told me. "Come out and jam with us. We can always use singers. You need to bring your own mic and amp, though."

I could feel my face turning red. "I'm not that great of a singer," I mumbled. "Just sort of okay."

Jeremy shrugged. "Doesn't matter. We're not about quality control in Jam Band."

"Dude, let's go." The drummer dragged his sticks down a trio of locker vents. "I've got things to do, people to see."

"Yeah, yeah, you're an important guy." Jeremy grabbed a drumstick and pointed it at us. "Definitely come out to jam sometime. We could use more girls."

We waited until the Jam Banders were out of earshot before we began to dissect what had just happened.

"I am so learning how to play the bass!" Sarah declared

to the hallway. "Not even Emma plays bass. It could totally be my thing."

"But why did you tell him I could sing?" I complained. "Because I can't, not really."

Sarah plucked a few strings of an invisible instrument "Oh, yes, you can. You just get too uptight when other people are listening to you. When it's just you fooling around, you sound great."

"But if I tried to sing with the Jam Band, other people would be listening," I pointed out.

"That's a problem," Sarah admitted. "But we'll figure something out. In the meantime, it's possible we've just encountered the cutest guy on the face of the planet."

And thus, our obsession with Jeremy Fitch was born. He was a junior, we soon learned from digging through last year's yearbook, and ran cross-country. And, as it turned out, his locker was just a few feet away from Ms. Morrison's classroom, so if we timed it just right, we had a daily chance encounter with the man of our dreams.

We always timed it just right.

"You got your bass yet?" Jeremy asks today when he sees me and Sarah making a beeline for his locker. "We sure could use you."

He says the same thing every day. His consistency is part of his charm.

"I'm still looking for one," Sarah tells him. "Only, I wish

somebody would make me a CD with really cool bass playing on it. You know, for inspiration."

"I'll get Monster to make you one," Jeremy says as he works his locker combination. "He lives to make the mix tape."

"Technically it would be a mix CD." As always, Sarah is constitutionally unable to keep herself from correcting a perceived error. "Or a tape," she amends quickly. "You say tomato, I say to-mah-to."

"I say avocado," Jeremy says, and bops Sarah on the head with his notebook. He turns. "What do you say, Motormouth? And when am I going to hear you sing?"

Before I can stammer out a reply, Jeremy slams shut his locker and is headed down the hallway. "Time to meander," he calls to us over his shoulder, which is how he always says good-bye.

Sometimes I think Sarah and I are way more into Jeremy Fitch than he's into us.

But that's just a theory.

We stand in silence for a moment, the way we always do after Jeremy's gone, letting whatever molecules he's breathed into the atmosphere during our brief time together settle over us. I allow myself to believe for a few lovely seconds that maybe high school isn't so awful after all, then await Sarah's daily critique.

"I shouldn't have said that about the mix CD, that was

the first thing I did wrong. Why am I always doing stuff like that? Why can't I just let things go?"

"Because you're a perfectionist," I suggest. "You can't help yourself."

Sarah sighs. "It's true, I can't."

And then she shakes it off. "Okay, number two. I should have insisted Jeremy make the mix tape, not this Monster guy. Can somebody's name really be Monster?"

"Probably a nickname," I tell her, moving out of the way for a skinny kid whose locker I'm blocking. "I mean nobody's going to name their kid 'Monster.' Nobody who's sane, anyway."

"They're crazy as loons," a voice booms. "That's a fact."

Sarah and I both jump. Standing in front of us—no, make that looming over us—is a Mack truck of a guy, six-two at the very least, in overalls and a tie-dyed T-shirt, his long red hair pulled into a ponytail. He shoves his hands in his pockets and leans back on his heels. "Monster Partin Monroe. It's right there on the birth certificate. I'll drive down to the county courthouse and get you a copy if you want."

"Um, no, that's okay," I tell him, feeling my cheeks go hot with embarrassment. "But, uh, why?"

"Why 'Monster'?"

I nod.

"You think I'm big now, you shoulda seen me when I

was born. Thirteen pounds, six ounces." Reaching out a long arm toward a locker a few feet to the left of me, he begins fiddling with the combination. "All my people are big. My grandaddy's big, my daddy's big, my mama's big. We are, genetically speaking, just a goodly sized people."

Sarah has seemingly been struck dumb for the last minute or so, but she finally finds her voice. "And do you play bass? Because Jeremy Fitch said you might make me a mix CD—uh, tape—of inspirational bass music."

"He did, huh?" Monster grins as he pulls a solitary notebook from his locker. "By inspirational, do you mean that which inspires you to visions of God and all his angels?"

"No," Sarah tells him. "I mean, music that will inspire me to play bass."

This seems to stop Monster Monroe right in his tracks. "You wanna play bass?"

Sarah nods. "For the Jam Band."

"Ain't that something?" Monster turns to me. "How 'bout you? You wanna play bass too?"

"Um, no," I say. "I was sort of thinking about singing, I mean with the Jam Band and everything, but I probably won't. I, uh, don't really like to sing in front of other people."

"You got to live bigger than that," Monster admonishes me. To Sarah he says, "I'll make you a mix. Teach you how to play bass, too, if you want. You got a bass already?"

"Not yet," Sarah says. "I don't actually know the first thing about finding a bass."

Monster looks at us appraisingly. "So we got a singer who don't really want to sing, and a bass player who don't know how to get her hands on a bass. Y'all need help."

Then he puts one hand on my shoulder and the other hand on Sarah's and leads us down the hallway, the crowds parting like the Red Sea before us.

Chapter Ten

The Ladies' Sewing Circle and Anarchist Cookbook Society

When I get home, Avery is sitting at the kitchen table, tears streaming down her cheeks, her favorite pink T-shirt in tatters on the table in front of her. My mom stands next to her, looking defeated, a copy of *Fabulous T-Shirt Makeovers* in her left hand, a pair of scissors in her right.

"I don't know what went wrong," she says with a sigh when she sees me. "The book made it all look so simple."

I put my backpack on a chair and pick up the shirt. It's nearly impossible to see what my mother was trying to do, other than completely destroy it. Sensing my confusion, my mom says, "You're supposed to cut off the bottom five inches and then sew a cute ribbon around the bottom of the remaining T-shirt and reattach the part of the T-shirt you've cut off by sewing it to the ribbon. Does that make sense?"

I squint, envision, and nod. "Yeah, I think so. Basically

you're inserting the ribbon as a band around the middle of the shirt."

"Exactly!" My mom brightens at being understood. Then she frowns again. "Only I guess these scissors aren't the best for cutting fabric." She holds up the scissors for my inspection. They're the ones she uses to cut pizza with. No wonder the shirt's in tatters.

"Yeah, unless your fabric's made out of, I don't know, steel wool," I say, unable to keep the sarcasm out of my voice.

My mom looks hurt. "They were the only scissors I could find."

"So do you want me to try to repair it?" I ask warily. It's not like I want to do the Bobbsey Twins any favors, but even I can't stand to watch a third grader cry.

Both my mom and Avery nod. Avery even manages a little smile and wipes a tear from her cheek. "I'll let you keep Bowser on your bed all week if you fix it, Janie."

Bowser is Avery's stuffed . . . something. I can't remember what Bowser used to be. All I know is that he's in even worse shape than Avery's shirt. "That's okay," I tell her, trying to sound nice about it. "You don't have to give me anything. I'm happy to help."

I pick up the various pieces of torn pink fabric, and my mom pulls some pink and green polka-dotted ribbon from a Jo-Ann's bag along with a spool of pink thread. "Do you want to try the treadle machine?" she asks.

“I’m fine,” I tell her, and head up the stairs to my room. In my closet, I find the old Singer sewing machine passed down to me by my grandmother when I was eight. I drag it out and set it up on my desk. It’s a pretty low-tech machine, but it works. For a long time I made easy things like A-line skirts and cotton/polyester blend tees, but now for the most part, I don’t make new clothes on my sewing machine, I re-create old ones. This past summer I went through a serious cuff stage, where I bought cool vintage fabric off of eBay and made roll-up cuffs for all my jeans and shorts. More recently, I’ve had a “What can you do with a thrift shop men’s shirt?” stage and an “Is it possible to make a skirt out of a T-shirt?” stage (the answer being yes, if you know how to put in an elastic waistband).

As I move around the scraps of Avery’s T-shirt like puzzle pieces, figuring out the best way to put them back together, I think about last year and how in my group of friends—Sarah, Lauren, Sonia, Rebecca, and the two Hannahs—I was known as the creative one because of the stuff I did with my clothes. Sarah had the girl genius and world-changer thing going on, Lauren wore the title of Total Jock, and Sonia and Rebecca were band geeks. The two Hannahs weren’t really known for anything, which was part of their charm. They were like fans who cheered the rest of us on.

In fact, it occurs to me as I’m pinning fabric together,

it's possible that out of everyone in my old group of friends I miss the Hannahs most of all. It was nice to come to school and have one Hannah or the other make a big deal out of my latest creation. It made me feel special.

Of course, nowadays I feel as special as a speck of dust. Sarah, who's the only one I see on a regular basis anymore, takes my clothes for granted. If I'm wearing a cool new pair of shoes, Sarah notices. A skirt I made out of an old pair of jeans and some killer fabric scraps? That's old news to Sarah. Nothing was old news to the Hannahs.

I sigh and begin to snip around the ragged edges of the shirt's hemline. In middle school, whenever I looked ahead to my high school years, I always saw myself in a crowd of friends. We were laughing and on our way somewhere—to the pep rally or a football game—or walking through South Pointe Mall en masse. In my daydreams, our group had expanded to include boys, cute, funny, smart boys, boys who liked to tease and cut up in a crowd but who, one-on-one, could be thoughtful and serious.

Instead who do I get?

Monster Monroe.

In the first two months of high school, Monster is the only guy who's paid me any attention at all. Well, there's Jeremy Fitch, but he doesn't really count. I'm not deluded enough to think that if Sarah and I stopped tracking Jeremy down at his locker, he would suddenly start showing up at ours. In fact, Jeremy has done an excellent job of being friendly without actually becoming a friend.

But as he walked me and Sarah down the C hallway this afternoon, Monster showed definite interest in being friends. He clearly didn't know about my alter ego, the odiferous Farm Girl, or if he did, he didn't care. He asked a ton of questions about what kind of music we listened to, shaking his head in violent disapproval at our vague answers. "Don't tell me you listen to everything or 'everything but country.' That don't mean nothing, and besides, what do you have against country music? I mean, what did Hank Williams ever do to you?"

And when we'd name bands, he wanted album titles, and when we named our favorite CDs, he wanted to know our favorite tracks.

By the time we got to the bus lanes, I was exhausted, but I definitely felt like Monster cared. Before he left us, he handed us his notebook and said, "Write your cell numbers in here, 'cause I might not be done asking you questions. If I'm gonna make you mix tapes, I got to know what I'm working with."

I took the notebook from him and dug a pen out of my backpack. "You're going to make me a mix tape too?"

"If you want to sing, you got to hear good singing. Judging by what you've just told me, I'm not convinced you have. Your mind's full of Top Forty pop radio crap. You can't learn to sing that way."

I wrote down my cell number and passed the notebook to Sarah. "But I told you, I'm not sure I really want to sing."

"What else you doing that's so important?"

Now, that's a good question. I sit down in front of the sewing machine, adjust the position of the foot pedal, and turn on the power. Maybe that's my problem, I think, as I put the spool of thread on the spindle and pull the line of thread through the needle. I'm not doing anything important. I can't even think of important things to do. I'm just Farm Girl, trailing the flotsam and jetsam of Green Acres behind me wherever I go. Really, all I want to do is live a normal life. I want to smell normal, look normal, act normal. I want to blend in. Why should that be such an unattainable goal?

Still, if I became that girl who sang on Fridays with the Jam Band, well, who knows where that might lead? Maybe I'll end up one of those famous singers who's always doing benefit events for important causes. I could do a Raising Awareness About Where Your Chocolate Comes From concert. At the very least, if I got the reputation as a Jam Band chick, maybe everybody in first period would forget about the day I came to school smelling like spoiled milk after Patsy Cline kicked the bucket over and soaked my socks thirty seconds before the bus driver started honking at the top of the driveway.

I mean, I could sing. Why not? Just because the first time Sarah and I stopped by the band room on a Friday after last period my voice froze in my throat before we even got to the door, it doesn't mean I can't sing. And just because the second Friday, when we swore this time we were going to go in and just watch the Jam Band, we chickened out at the last minute, that doesn't mean I can't sing either.

I just have to practice, that's all. I'll listen to Monster's mix tape and learn. I'll sing along with the singers and then turn off the CD and sing alone.

Once I get famous for my singing, then people will flock around me, asking me to join their clubs and come to their parties, and high school will be in the bag. Who knows, maybe I could convince my parents to move back into town, where I could live the normal teenage life of my dreams.

Before I drift too far off into never-never land, I press my foot to the pedal and start hemming Avery's shirt.

My cell vibrates in my pocket. I can hear Sarah's excitement before she even starts talking. "You have to come to dinner tonight!" she exclaims before I get the second syllable of "hello" out of my mouth.

"Um, okay," I say. "But why?"

"So we can convince Emma to work on this project! My mom is totally into Emma helping us. She thinks it'll get Emma back on the right path."

"To where?"

"Who knows? Harvard, I guess. Or at least community college. Anywhere but a Harley-Davidson convention."

It's weird to think that after all these years we'll finally be doing something with Emma—by which I mean, doing something that might actually involve personal interaction and dialogue. Sarah, Emma, and I have done stuff together—we've gone in the Lymans' minivan to shopping malls and state fairs and movie theaters—but even though Emma was with us, she wasn't really *with* us. Even when we were in first grade and Emma was in fourth, she seemed to be orbiting around her family instead of living inside of it.

Did she have friends when she was younger? I try to think of who Emma sat on the bus with when we all went to Sewall Elementary, but every picture my mind calls up is of Emma with her nose in a book—on the bus, on the playground, and walking down the hall. It wasn't until she was in middle school that Emma started to be known for her interesting friendships, always with older kids, the kind your parents start warning you away from as early as third grade.

Sometimes when Emma was out doing who knows what

with who knows who, Sarah and I would sneak into her room. It was surprisingly neat, with four tall bookshelves filled with books, and a desk free of clutter. "It's how she gets away with so much," Sarah told me once. "In our house, neatness counts for a lot."

In middle school Emma kept a journal, which we found shoved underneath her pillow and of course read. We were in fifth grade and Emma was in eighth, and we figured Emma's journal would be full of good stuff—stuff about boys and bras and periods (our obsessions at the time). Instead she'd written page after page about God. Did God exist? If God didn't exist, what set the universe in motion? If God was good, why was there so much suffering? If only one religion was the right religion, wouldn't God have done a better job of making that clear to everyone?

In other words, Emma's diary was a huge disappointment. But later, when she stopped just being Emma, Sarah's big sister, and became Emma Lyman, Famous Wild Child, I thought about all that stuff she'd written about when she was thirteen. Did she give up on God, or just the opposite? The minute Emma got her own car, she'd put a bumper sticker on it that read LIVE LARGE, and it occurred to me that if there is a God, that's something He might want us to do.

So Emma lives large, but she lives in Emma World. Now, finally, maybe she's going to take a step into Sarah and Janie World. It actually makes me sort of nervous, but I don't mention this to Sarah, who has finally wound down about the project and has started on our new friendship with Monster Monroe.

"He's cute, don't you think? Not my type, but I could see how he could be somebody else's type. I can't believe he's going to teach me how to play bass. I wonder what his house is like."

Next Monday, after school, Monster is taking us to what he referred to as his "digs," which are on the other side of Manneville, where he's going to lend Sarah an old bass of his and teach her how to play. No matter how hard I try, I can't envision the house that Monster Monroe might live in. He's just too big for a house. An airplane hangar seems more the right size.

Avery appears at my doorway. "Are you done with my shirt?" she whispers, leaning into my room, but not actually crossing the threshold.

"Almost," I whisper back, and Avery gives me a thumbs-up and scoots back down the hallway. I wonder if she looks up to me the way Sarah looks up to Emma. I don't think so, at least not yet, and definitely not with my new bad attitude. Right now my mom is the big star in Avery's world.

My glance falls on the pink T-shirt on my desk, its various scraps held together by pins. Yeah, my mom's the center attraction now, but one more T-shirt disaster like this one, and her big-star days might be over.

Chapter Eleven

A Night in the Suburbs

I sneak a glance at my mom's expression as she steers the car onto Victoria Lane. Is there any sign of regret? A flicker of nostalgia for our days in suburbia, where mowing the lawn only takes twenty minutes? Does she miss her old neighbors, not just the Lymans, but the Bowermans and the Lees, the Pauls and the Grahams? Now her only neighbors are chickens and goats, and I can vouch for the fact that they never throw block parties.

But my mom seems lost in thought, which probably means she's mentally composing her next blog post as opposed to mourning her suburban past. I bet it'll start, "I was driving through my old neighborhood the other day . . ." and will contain all sorts of musings about how she's found herself on the farm. Which, okay, she sort of has. Back when we lived on Victoria Lane, my mom was stressed out a lot. She had work, she had preschool board meetings, she had bad dinners to prepare, and two little kids to get to bed. She drank a lot of wine at dinner and ranted about property taxes and what an idiot her editor was. Now she hardly drinks at all, unless she's had a particularly egregious crafting disaster, and she's her own editor.

When we pull up to the curb in front of Sarah's house, we both look across the street to our old house. As I've done on more than one occasion since starting high school, I imagine what my life would be like if every morning found me strolling leisurely down Victoria Lane to the bus stop on the corner instead of scampering through a minefield of animal droppings and other farmyard hazards. I'd get on the bus and not one person would feel the need to yell, "It's Skunk Girl! Everybody plug your noses!"

I turn and stare out the windshield. It suddenly occurs to me how sad this is—that in only two months' time I've gone from a girl who daydreamed about running for student council and joining the yearbook staff to someone who fantasizes about blending in so thoroughly that everyone forgets she exists.

I don't bother knocking on the Lymans' door; I just go right in. "I'm here!" I yell from the front hallway, and this feels so good to say, I say it again. "I'm here! What's for dinner?"

"Pot roast!" Mrs. Lyman calls. "Tell your mom when you

go home that I made it with locally grown beef."

I poke my head into the kitchen. "Have you been reading her blog?"

"Religiously," Mrs. Lyman reports. "I like reading it out loud to Henry. You should see the steam coming out of his ears when your mom writes about sustainable development!"

Sarah's in her room, working on her laptop. "Did you know Mr. Pritchard is famous?" she asks me as I flop down on her bed. "Emma's the one who told me, actually. She's read all about him."

"Have you asked her to help us with the project?"

Sarah shakes her head no. "But I'm getting her interested. She was actually impressed that you knew Mr. Pritchard. When I told her about Mrs. Pritchard helping people learn to read and write so they could vote, her eyes practically popped out of her head. She was totally into it."

I can't help but grin. Emma's impressed that I know Mr. Pritchard. Suddenly I feel like a star. "I'll tell her all about him at dinner. Maybe we could take her over to the nursing home so she could meet him."

Sarah holds up a hand. "Let me be the one to drop that little morsel of incentive," she tells me. "With Emma, it's all about the timing."

At dinner Mr. Lyman quizzes me about my grades, concerned that I'm not doing all that well in Algebra I. "This is the year it all starts to count, Janie," he lectures. "You've always been a great student. Don't let the high school social scene distract you."

Sarah rolls her eyes, and I try not to giggle. I don't know what strikes me as funnier, the phrase "high school social scene" or the idea that I might be a part of it.

"Learning to socialize is an important part of an education," Emma points out to her father. "Grades aren't everything."

Mr. Lyman pointedly ignores her. A tension falls over the table, as though Emma opening her mouth has violated some rule of etiquette. This is the part I don't like about eating with the Lymans—they are not a relaxed people. At my house, things are pretty laid-back at the dinner table. My dad jokes and tells stories, my mom gives the farm report, and Avery always has something adorable to say about life in the third grade. Even on those occasions where I can't bring myself to contribute one word to the discussion and Avery's adorability scrapes on my last nerve, I sort of enjoy hanging out. The food's good, and nobody calls me Skunk Girl.

I feel totally awkward, sitting here in the Lyman family's prickly silence. "So Emma," I blurt out when I can't take it any longer, "do you want to meet Mr. Pritchard?"

Sarah glares at me, but Emma looks interested. "How do you know him, anyway?"

So I explain about my dad's latest oral history project and Mr. Pritchard's yard art. "I've seen the cross a couple of times," I say, sounding like a ten-year-old bragging about her latest trip to Disney World. "It's really cool. In the summer, there are flowers blooming all over it."

"It sounds obscene!" Mr. Lyman declares. "A burnt cross in your yard. It should have been taken down as soon as the flames were put out."

"I think it sounds amazing," Emma says quietly. "Totally amazing."

The sudden sound of a motorcycle engine revving out on the driveway spurs everybody into action. "Time to head upstairs," Emma says, pushing her chair away from the table with a loud scrape.

Mr. Lyman throws down his napkin. "No, you're not, Emma! I told you I was going to call the police the next time he showed up."

Mrs. Lyman stands and picks up her plate. "Another dinner ruined," she says with a sigh. "Oh, well, I do think the local beef really is better." She turns to me. "Tell your mom I said so."

"Follow me!" Sarah grabs my arm and pulls me into the living room, where she presses her face against the window. "There's Todd!" she says, signaling for me to look too. "He does this almost every night."

"Is your dad going to call the police?" I ask, looking out

the window at Emma's boyfriend, who is standing in the shadow of the garage and looking up in the direction of Emma's room. He laughs at something Emma calls down to him, then blows her a kiss.

"No, although he always says he's going to. Trust me, there's already been one big scene in our front yard. My dad doesn't want another one."

We head back into the kitchen, where we help Mrs. Lyman clear the table and volunteer to do the dishes. "So, when are you going to ask Emma if she wants to help us?" I ask Sarah as I scrub grease off the stovetop. "We probably should get to work pretty soon."

"Well, I was thinking, maybe she could give you a ride home tonight," Sarah says in a sort of dreamy voice. "And I could go too, and then we could—"

"Not going to happen," Mrs. Lyman says from the other side of the kitchen counter, where she's sorting through the day's mail. "I'll take Janie home. The way things are going, your father won't let Emma out of the house until graduation."

"Could Emma come along for the ride?" Sarah asked hopefully. "Or, you know, maybe she could be the one who drives us around for our project? We need someone to drive us, right? And you and Dad don't have time, and it would help us get a good grade."

Mrs. Lyman considers this. "Your dad might let Emma

drive you for your project. Emphasis on the word 'might.' We should probably underplay the fact that the project is for a women's studies class, however."

"Good thinking, Mom," Sarah says, smiling at Mrs. Lyman, who smiles back and says, "Well, that's what they pay me for."

I scrub harder at the spot on the stove, trying not to be jealous of how well Sarah and her mom get along. Oh, they have their disagreements and their bad days, and Sarah's very vocal about her mother's insufficiencies as a recycler, but in general they like each other. Maybe they have to, since Mr. Lyman and Emma so clearly don't. Maybe you need at least one stable parent-child relationship in every family for the whole thing not to collapse.

Sarah comes over and squeezes my arm. "If my parents let Emma drive," she whispers, "then she's in the bag, believe you me."

I smile at her and imagine driving around town in Emma's VW. That's one way not to blend in, I tell myself, and then I can't decide if I find that idea exciting or absolutely terrifying.

Chapter Twelve

The Rock 'n' Roll Diaries: An Afterschool Special

A week and a half into our gig as library buddies, Verbena and I are actually discussing whether or not we should venture out of the library and into the cafeteria. We discuss this in whispers, as if it's too scary a subject to give full voice to.

"It's the only way we're going to get ourselves out there," Verbena insists in a hushed tone. "In the public eye. I mean, there are people in this school who are like us, who'll want to be friends with us, if they just know we're alive."

"Or forget what they know," I add, wishing I could go back to the beginning days of school and start over. You can bet that clump of goat manure wouldn't have made it past the goat pen, much less onto the bus and into local folkore.

The funny thing is, now that I'm friends with Verbena,

I feel like a social success story, with two spots in my day—lunch and Great Girls and Women—where I have someone to talk to. That's a 100 percent increase from two weeks ago. And if you count Monster—and since I've now actually been to his house and eaten from his snack supply, I do—well, hey, I'm practically the prom queen.

Still, I get Verbena's point. Lunch is supposed to be a time for mixing and mingling among one's peers. Impossible to do if you're an island of one, but conceivable when there are two of you.

Verbena, it turns out, is new. "I'm always new," she complained to me during our second library lunch together, digging out a bag of carrot sticks from her purse, a blue pleather pouch that matched her blue go-go boots. "My mom's company keeps relocating her every two years. She goes to new divisions, fixes whatever's wrong with them, rearranges the management, gets the employees a better brand of doughnuts for the break room, and then moves on to the next place. *We* move on to the next place."

She held out a carrot stick to me, but I shook my head. For reasons I cannot fathom, Verbena is exempt from Mrs. Welsch's rules, but every time I do anything remotely suspicious—rummage through my backpack for a pen, walk up to the front desk to grab a Kleenex—Mrs. Welsch narrows her eyes at me as though she expects me to use the pen to scrawl all over her books or tear the tissue into spitwad-size pieces to stick under her tables.

"What does your dad do?" I asked, watching with interest as Verbena took the tiniest bites possible from a carrot stick. At the rate she was going, this one would last her until the weekend.

Verbena rolled her eyes. "He writes murder mysteries. He doesn't publish them, he just writes them."

"Does he try to publish them?"

"Of course he tries to publish them. The problem is, they're not any good. My dad is really squeamish about blood and violence, so all his murders are boring. And his so-called sleuth is an accountant, which is what my dad used to be. But when my mom started making so much money, he quit his job to write."

She chewed thoughtfully for a moment, then said, "Moving so much when I was little didn't matter. Little kids will make friends with you in a minute. But it gets harder every year. In fact, I'm thinking about divorcing my parents, just so I can stop moving. The damage it's done to my social life is overwhelming."

I decided against pointing out that having skulls and crossbones inked up and down her forearms—that day's particular Sharpie tattoo theme—might also work against the cultivation of a vibrant social life.

Today Verbena's tattoos are a little more subdued. She's in a literary mood, apparently, and has been writing words and phrases on her left arm—COWABUNGA! LIFE SUCKS! PEACHY KEEN! YOWZA! BIG BULLY!—in a straight line from her wrist to the inside of her elbow.

"It's not like I want to be popular," Verbena insists. "I just want to have a group. I've always wanted to be in a group." She stops, leans back, and gives me a long, assessing look. "Why aren't you in a group? Is it your clothes?"

I look down at what I'm wearing: a black scoop-neck T-shirt and a vintage A-line yellow skirt I've appliquéd with red flannel cowboy boots, a perfectly respectable ensemble. "Is there something wrong with my clothes?"

Verbena crosses her hands over her heart and looks very sincere. "I personally love them, but then I'm the creative type. And I appreciate creativity in other people. But not everyone does, right?"

I suppose this is true. And it's not like I've never gotten snide comments. But for the most part, people either think what I wear is cool or they don't seem to notice it.

Besides, I remind myself, I have a group of friends. I just never see most of them anymore. "The problem is," I explain to Verbena, "the group I was in all through middle school got split up this year. The only one I ever get to hang out with at school is my best friend, Sarah."

Verbena winces at the phrase "best friend." "You're so lucky," she says after being quiet for a minute. "Whenever I get to a new place, all the good best friends are taken."

I don't know what to say, so I start telling her about Sarah, what she's like, what her interests are, her obsession with ethical chocolate. I notice after I've gone on a few minutes that Verbena is frowning, and I wonder if I've somehow hurt her feelings by describing one of my friends when she doesn't have any, if you don't count me.

"Did I say something wrong? Maybe I shouldn't be talking about my best friend since you don't exactly—uh—have one, I guess."

Verbena examines the Lite 'n' Rite parmesan bread stick she's pulled out of a box from her purse, then takes a bite before answering. "No, no. It's just this Sarah person—I don't know, she sounds kind of . . . something. Like an overachiever type, I guess."

"Well, she is, sort of," I admit. "She's just really smart. She likes to have a lot going on."

"But you're not like that."

For some reason, that stings. I used to be an overachiever, I'm pretty sure, or at the very least part of the smart-girl group, the straight-A team. Is there something about me that suggests I'm no longer living up to my potential? I sniff the air around me, checking for that telltale sour milk smell, but all I get a whiff of is parmesan bread stick and library paste. "You've only known me a little while," I complain to Verbena. "For all you know, I could be writing some major magnum opus, or curing cancer in my basement when I'm done with my homework."

"You could be," Verbena replies, pointing her bread stick at me. "But you're not. This Sarah person, on the other hand, is probably working on a cure for cancer and the common cold and—oh, I don't know. Rabies or something."

It's funny, hearing someone else's take on Sarah, someone who's judging her solely on my description. I feel sort of guilty, both for unintentionally painting a picture of Sarah that turned out to be less than flattering, and also for enjoying Verbena's negative opinion. The fact is, Sarah *is* an overachiever—and a know-it-all, and, as I told her in no uncertain terms when we were seven, a bossy-boss.

And, if I'm completely honest, she can get on my nerves. Like this Monday, with Monster. She was treating him like a Jeremy Fitch tutorial. Driving to Monster's house in his truck—red, ancient, frighteningly rusted—she interrogated Monster about everything Jeremy.

"So what kind of girl would you say he likes? Intelligent, athletic, artsy?" Sarah asked, sounding like she was reading from a quiz in a magazine. "Vivacious, quiet, articulate?"

"I think he likes girls, period," Monster told her, grinning. "I never noticed him being particular about it."

"But there's got to be some special kind of girl—his dream girl, right?"

Monster guffawed. "Dream girl? Ain't such a thing.

You walk, you talk, you got mammary glands, well, that's gonna do it right there for most guys."

"You're not very romantic, are you?" Sarah plucked a small purple rubber frog from a collection of rubber frogs on the dashboard and stretched one of its legs so it was pointing accusingly at Monster. "I can't believe that guys don't have particular things they want in a girl."

"They want mammary glands. *Pronounced* mammary glands."

"I bet he likes smart girls." Sarah brightened. "Musicians like smart girls, don't they? Look at John Lennon and Yoko Ono."

"Oh, yeah, musicians are known for bird-dogging intelligent women," Monster mockingly agreed. "I hear Elvis had a big thing for Madame Curie."

The conversation petered out after that. Sarah fiddled with the radio, which only seemed to receive static, and I examined the menagerie of critters littering Monster's dash—besides the frogs, there were several tiny cows, apparently glued down, and a passel of three-inch-high dinosaurs in alarming hues, purples, reds, and one striped brontosaurus—wondering what on earth were we doing. Frankly, I was beginning to question Sarah's sanity. I mean, did she really think Jeremy Fitch was going to fall for her—for her mind? Or because she was nice, or up-to-date on current events?

Or because she played the bass?

The Jam Band idea seemed crazier to me every time I thought about it. I could understand why we'd gotten so excited about it at first. Being in a band is one of those notions that sort of seizes you. It's like when you're a kid and decide to put on a play or have a carnival in your backyard. You spend forty-eight to seventy-two crazed hours devoting your every waking minute to making it happen, and then, *poof,* all of a sudden you run out of steam and your big idea dies a quiet death while you sit in front of the TV watching ancient *Saved by the Bell* episodes.

I had a feeling Jam Band didn't have much longer to live either.

Half a mile past the Wal-Mart, Monster pulled the truck into the parking lot of what looked like an old motel, an L-shaped, two-story building, an empty pool in front filled with burger-joint trash and two decrepit beach loungers. "Well, ladies, we're here," he announced as the engine grumbled and lurched to a halt.

"You live here?" Sarah sounded shocked. "I mean, for real? With your family?"

Monster pushed open his door (the handle didn't actually work, but brute strength seemed to do the trick), got out of the truck, then leaned his head back in. "Not with my family, no way. I think I mentioned to you that they're pretty nuts. Mama and Daddy, anyway. Granny's all right.

End of last summer I said, 'What do y'all think about me moving out?' and they said fine. I found this place, and Daddy came over and signed the lease, helped me move my stuff in. I pay the rent, but Granny usually slips me a twenty to help with the utilities."

He checked his watch. "In fact, I got to be at work by six, so we better get this party started."

We followed him up the rickety staircase to the second floor. "This used to be a Motel 6," he explained as he inserted a key into a door with 227-28 scrawled in marker on it. "But then they built a new Motel 6 over by the highway and sold this one to my landlord, Morris."

Monster opened the door and gallantly stepped back to let us enter. "Ladies, welcome to my den of iniquity. Or at least I'm hoping that's what it's gonna be one day. I'm working up to that stage incrementally."

Monster's apartment consisted of two hotel rooms connected by a bathroom. He led us quickly through the first room—room 227, I guessed, which consisted mostly of an unmade queen-size bed, a dresser, and a TV with rabbit-ear antennas taped to the top—through the bathroom, where a coffee mug and a cereal bowl were laid out to dry on overlapping brown paper towels next to the sink, and into room 228, where there was a couch instead of a bed and a mini-fridge with a hot plate on top.

"Sleep in one room, live in the other," he declared,

knocking a bunch of magazines off the couch and motioning for us to sit. "Don't ever mix the two. It cost me a little extra to rent a suite, but it's worth it. I can't abide eating in the same room I sleep in."

Monster's living room appeared to be a shrine to all things musical. I counted nine different guitars, all types, a trumpet, a violin, and five amps, not to mention a snake's nest worth of cords slithering over every spare inch of carpet. A humongous boom box was set against the wall across from the couch, and a line of CD cases—there had to be at least two hundred—stretched along the baseboard of another wall.

Monster lifted a red bass from its stand and held it in front of us. "Now, here's what you got to understand about the bass. It is a rhythm instrument that, unlike the drum kit, its partner in crime, can carry a tune. The bass guitar gets taken for granted outside the world of jazz and funk, but don't let that fool you. Ain't no such thing as rock and roll without the bass."

He handed the bass to Sarah, who took it from him and held it awkwardly in her lap. "Now, I'm gonna find you a strap, and then we'll get you plugged in and see what kinda stuff you got."

Rummaging through a box next to the couch, Monster pulled out a thick black strap with neon yellow peace signs running up and down its length. "This oughta do ya," he said, leaning over Sarah and attaching the strap to the bass. "We'll adjust it so the bass ain't hanging too low. Why don't you go ahead and stand up, give me something to work with here."

Sarah stood, clutching the neck of the bass in one hand and grabbing onto the body with the other. "Relax," Monster told her, give the strap a yank. "You can't be uptight and play bass. Contradiction in terms."

"It doesn't feel comfortable," Sarah complained, tugging at the strap where it crossed her shoulder. "And it's heavy. How am I supposed to hold it for more than five minutes?"

"You'll get used to it," Monster assured her. He stepped back to examine her. "You're kinda little for a bass player, it's true. Lotta times you go see a band, the bass player's the big guy. Even the girl bass players—you guys know Tina Wannamaker, plays bass for Evermore? She's a pretty tall drink of water."

Sarah stood in front of the couch, looking miserable, the bass dangling close to her knees. *Here it is,* I thought. *Here's where the Jam Band dream dies.*

As if reading my mind, Sarah turned to me and said, "Maybe I should try out for cross-country."

"Maybe," I agreed. Not that I thought running cross-country would win her a place in Jeremy Fitch's heart either, but you can't stomp all over a person's hopes and desires and expect her to stay your best friend.

Sarah shrugged off the bass and held it out to Monster. "I don't think this is going to work out, but thanks."

Monster looked confused. "You didn't even plug it in yet."

"It's just too uncomfortable. And you're right, I'm probably too short to play."

Monster grabbed the bass by the neck. He turned to me. "Well, you're on the tall side. Why don't you give it a try?"

"I don't know anything about playing bass," I told him, but even as the words came out of my mouth I was reaching for it. "I mean, I guess I could try, but don't expect anything great."

Sarah looked concerned. "I'm not so sure this is a good idea, Janie. You've never even played piano."

I pulled the strap over my head and balanced the bass against my hips. "What's that got to do with anything?"

"Nothing, I guess," Sarah admitted. "I guess I just don't see you as the musician type."

"And you are?" I felt my face getting hot. Sarah was just being Sarah, offering her considered if unsolicited opinions, but suddenly Sarah being Sarah was starting to irritate me.

"Maybe I'll be a great bass player," I told her as Monster plugged a cord into an amp and led it over to where I was standing. "Maybe I'll be the—the—Tina Wannamaker of Manneville High."

"Strictly speaking, Tina Wannamaker is the Tina Wannamaker of Manneville High," Monster said, plugging the other end of the amp cord into the bass. "She's a senior. Evermore's a local band. Don't you keep up with the local music scene?"

"We're really not that into music," Sarah informed him. "We were just trying it out for a little while."

Before Monster could respond—and I could see that the response forming on his lips wasn't going to be pretty—I plucked a string. It was the bottom string—the E string, I'd learn in a minute—and it vibrated all the way up my arm.

It sounded—and felt—incredibly cool.

Monster turned away from Sarah. "That's good. Now put your pointer finger on the second string, first fret, and play that."

I did as I was told.

It sounded even cooler.

And all of a sudden, I felt larger. Not taller, not heavier, not physically bigger. Larger on the inside. Like suddenly—how do I say this?—I felt like life had possibilities I hadn't been aware of five seconds before.

All this from playing two notes on Monster's bass.

◆ ◆ ◆

Sitting in the library across the table from Verbena, I can still feel the reverb running up and down my arms. And I can still see the bored expression on Sarah's face as Monster taught me to play an easy Ramones song.

Which is just my luck. When I finally get excited about something, Sarah couldn't be less interested. Standing in the middle of Monster's apartment, I didn't know whether to scream or cry. I mean, how many times had I hopped on Sarah's latest bandwagon? How many times had I helped her get petitions signed and posters hung up?

And she gives up on Jam Band just when I figure out it's something I really want to do?

"Sarah's great," I tell Verbena. "I mean, we've been best friends since first grade. She's totally cool. She just, I don't know, knows her own mind. She's got her own opinions. She—"

And then I stop, because it hits me that I'm not sure if I'm trying to convince Verbena of Sarah's greatness, or if I'm trying to convince myself.

Chapter Thirteen

Future Shock

Riding the bus back to Farm World this afternoon, it occurs to me that I'm on the verge of having an almost normal life, one with friends and activities and everything. When I got on the bus after the last bell, not one single person yelled out, "Skunk girl!" I looked around for a few seconds waiting for it, and then Steve told me to find a seat before he found one for me. So I did.

Even before that, it had been an interesting day. For instance, in art, pale Meg finally spoke to me. Well, first she dropped a rock on the table in front of me, and then she spoke. "This might help," she said before heading to her corner. "Stones are elemental and beautiful. They're everyday objects and they're art."

I had to admit, for a rock, it was pretty darn cute. And frankly, I could use all the inspiration I could get. The collage thing was not happening for me. I was trying. I'd ruined three canvases gluing stuff to them, No. 2 pencils and gum wrappers and a used-up tube of lipstick I'd found in the bottom of my backpack. But the junk I stuck on the canvases just sat there, like it was wondering why it wasn't in a trash can where it belonged. I couldn't bring myself to take Sarah's words out of the envelope in my backpack, or the picture of the Pritchards. I didn't want to ruin them.

I put a fresh canvas on the table in front of me and put the rock in the middle of it. I was pretty sure the rock was quartz, if my seventh-grade earth science knowledge still served; it was white with pink streaks running through it. One side was perfectly smooth, as if the edges and points had been sheared off. I liked how it looked feminine and masculine at the same time.

I walked over to Meg's corner. "Thanks for the rock," I told her. "Unfortunately, I don't know what to do with it."

"If you like it, live with it a little while," Meg suggested. "Look around for other things that remind you of it, or have some sort of intuitive connection for you."

I glanced at the collage she was working on. She had glued jar lids and bottle caps over a large canvas—I noted a Gerber baby food jar lid and a Duke's Mayonnaise jar lid and at least five Pepsi bottle caps—and had drawn orange and red concentric circles around each one so that her collage was practically pulsating.

"That's really cool," I told her. "I wish I could think of something like that."

"You will," said Meg. "You just need to relax a little."

So I spent the rest of the class trying to relax, which was hard to do, as Chester and Lynnette were deeply involved in a thumb-wrestling tournament, but nothing came to me. The rock was pretty, but what could I do except maybe glue some more rocks next to it? Turn it into a science project? Drill holes and make a necklace?

And then, on my way to Great Girls and Women, I spotted a tiny paper parasol, the kind you get in fancy drinks, underneath the water fountain outside of the girls' bathroom, the fountain that spits out warm water and is always clogged with gum, so nobody ever uses it. The parasol was pink and had tiny violet flowers painted on it. I took Meg's rock out of my pocket and held it next to the parasol.

It was a match made in heaven. For the first time since Ms. Ashdown had introduced me to the insanity that was a Robert Rauschenberg collage, I thought maybe I could make this art thing work.

And this afternoon I had another glimpse of what having an almost normal life might be like, after the last bell, walking toward the bus line with Monster while he explained the contents of the CD he'd just handed me ("Lots of simple stuff—easy Strokes, some Rage Against the Machine, a couple of early Police tunes—just listen and try to play it by ear"). It seemed like every other person we passed had something to say—a "Yo, Monsterman" or a "Hey, dude," and even one "Yo, Monster and the chick Monster's walking with." I felt warm and fuzzy with the sense of being included, even if I had no idea who these people were or how they got their parents' permission for all the tattoos.

But I was also intensely aware that Sarah wasn't walking with us. After our Jeremy Fitch moment (which was awkward, what with Sarah sticking to the same old script but clearly uncomfortable speaking her lines), she turned to me to begin the daily analysis, but before she could get started, Monster was standing behind us, wanting to know if I'd practiced any at home on the bass he'd lent me and holding out a CD he'd made for me to listen to. Before I knew it, Sarah had disappeared, and it was just me and Monster.

I kept looking at him sideways as we made our way down the hall, wondering why some people could totally be themselves and still be accepted by everyone, while other people—people who did everything in the world to fit in—were shunned like the runts of the litter. Walking next to Monster, I could only hope some of his mojo might rub off on me.

"So, okay, yeah, things are definitely better at school," I

tell Loretta Lynn as I freshen up the water in her pen after I've had a snack and changed into Farm World apparel. "I think people have completely forgotten about the goat poop incident."

Loretta Lynn gives me a hurt look.

"No offense," I tell her. "It really doesn't stink at all. People are just—well, funny about poop, I guess."

Believe me, I would know.

My sense that things are looking up seems especially true ten minutes later when I sit down at the kitchen table to check my Facebook page on Mom's MacBook and see that I have a message from Emma, a definite first.

I hear you and Monster Monroe have a thing going on, the message begins, sans greeting. *Who knew you were cool? So: Saturday. See if you can get us to see H.P. after lunch. I've got questions, I need answers.*

Who said anything about me and Monster Monroe? Sarah? But she would know there's nothing going on. So it must have been someone else.

I lean back in my chair, relishing the thought that there might be a rumor about me floating around school. An untrue rumor, granted, but a rumor nonetheless, and one that makes me seem kind of cool. I start to reach for the phone, which is resting on the pile of this morning's papers, to call Sarah and see if together we can get to the bottom of this, but more to the point to have an opportunity to bask in this brief, tiny moment of Janie Gorman glory. A false rumor flying through the halls in my name!

Sweet.

So what stops me from picking up the phone? Sarah's disappearing act this afternoon after Monster showed up? The thought she might pooh-pooh the very notion that tongues are wagging about me and Monster? Sort of kind of. But more than that . . .

I guess I'm afraid she's a little mad at me, and I'm a little mad at her, only neither of us is mad for any real reason. I've seen it happen before with other girls—friendships that dissolved for no apparent cause or that just went bust because one friend decided to join band and the other friend joined Drama Club and their paths never crossed again.

That couldn't happen to me and Sarah. Could it?

No, it can't. If nothing else, we have a big project to do. A big project will bring us back together, no problem.

Not that we've broken apart. Not us.

So instead of dialing Sarah's number, I dial the number for Pine Manor Assisted Living Estates and ask for Mr. Harlan Pritchard.

"You want to come talk to me about Mrs. Pritchard?" Mr. Pritchard asks in his raspy voice when I tell him about the project. "About the Freedom School?"

"Freedom School?" I haven't heard anything about a

Freedom School, but a little buzz of excitement tingles along my spine at the sound of those two words put together. Whatever a Freedom School is, it's got to be a lot better than the deal they've got going on at Manneville High.

"That's what they called it," Mr. Pritchard explains. "Well, officially it was called a citizenship school, but folks got to calling it Freedom School. Hazel and Septima started it back in 1961. Septima Brown, that's who taught with Hazel. She still lives in Manneville, if you girls want to visit with her. In fact, how 'bout we all ride over next Saturday? It's been a long time since I paid Septima a visit."

Me, Sarah, Mr. Pritchard, and Emma all riding to town in Emma's baby blue VW bug.

How could I say no?

"Now tell me what that daddy of yours is up to," Mr. Pritchard says, and I can almost hear him relaxing in his chair, getting ready to shoot the breeze, which we shoot for the next forty-five minutes. When I finally get off the phone I feel oddly refreshed, like I've just returned from a hike in the woods on a cool autumn afternoon. For a full five minutes I sit at the kitchen table, completely satisfied with my life.

Then, with the ferocity and high-speed winds of a hurricane, my mom rushes into the kitchen and announces,

"Put it on your calendar! We're going to have a hootenanny!"

And even though I have no idea what a hootenanny is, I already know it's going to ruin everything.

Chapter Fourteen

In Which My Mother Totally Loses It Once and for All

By 9 p.m., my mom has updated her blog to let the whole world know that in three weeks we will be hosting a humongous outdoor party on our mini-farm, and all her readers are invited.

By 10 p.m., her old editor at the *Manneville Gazette,* Maura Gibbs, having read my mom's blog, has IM'd her with a request for a feature-length article to run the week before the party.

By 10:15 p.m., my mom has informed me that I should invite all my friends, promising we will have a rip-roaring good time.

By 10:16 p.m., I have informed my mom that I plan to be in New Zealand on the day of the hootenanny, or at least spending the night at Sarah's.

By 10:18 p.m., my mom is complaining to my dad that she doesn't know what's happened to the old

Janie, who was so enthusiastic about everything.

By 10:18:32 p.m., I have stomped upstairs, muttering how I don't understand why my mother is so insistent on ruining my life.

I mean, imagine it. Your mother is inviting the whole community to your backyard to eat hot dogs and sing folk songs. Bring your beat-up guitars, your whining fiddles, your world-weary mandolins, your honkin' harmonicas! Bring your overalls, your bandanna-wearing dogs, your hayseeds, your green-life Porta-Potties! Bring your homemade bread and lentil stew and wheat germ brownies! We're gonna have us a good ol' time down on the farm.

It's over the top, you've got to admit.

After I stew a little while, sitting on my bed and plucking the strings of the bass Monster's given me to practice on, I realize it's not the gathering of the Whole Foods tribes I mind so much, it's the publicity. It's being identified with the Farm Freak Family that bugs me. I know a lot of kids who wouldn't mind at all: crunchy granola types who hang out on the school steps every morning kicking around a Hacky Sack, the eco kids who wear sandals made from tires and gossip about global warming under a birch tree near the flagpole every morning, any vegan worth his or her salt. No offense, free country and everything, but I have spent the last two and a half months trying to distance myself as far from my Farm Girl identity as possible.

I remind myself that no one I know reads the paper, not even online. I mean, not even the adults, other than my parents. The circulation can't be more than five thousand. I also remind myself that no one actually knows my name outside a circle of twenty people. I'm making too big a deal out of this.

I just wish I had fifteen minutes to get my life together before my mom comes up with yet another scheme to throw me off my game. First it's the homemade wardrobe, now it's the hippie-dippy back-to-basics sing-along. Next she'll be investing in a printing press so we can hand out leaflets calling for mandatory composting toilets in every house in Manneville.

No one knows you're related, I tell myself, taking in deep, calming breaths. *No one has any idea.*

"I read your mother's blog this morning," Mrs. Welsch tells me when I walk into the library Wednesday at lunchtime. "She's such an interesting woman. I bought a chicken because of her. Sadly, a rat ate it, but I may buy another someday."

"A rat ate it?"

"It was a rather small chicken. Of course, then a snake ate the rat, and I didn't know whether to be happy or in fear for my life. Your mother never mentioned that chickens draw rats, and rats draw snakes."

"You have to keep the feed inside the house," I inform her. "Like you would dog food."

Mrs. Welch's eyes widen. "Ahhhh, very interesting. In any event, should I RSVP in a formal way to your mother, or just leave a comment on her blog?"

"You're coming?" I catch myself from staggering back into the copier.

"I play a mean twelve-string guitar," Mrs. Welsch says, and then she winks and gives me the thumbs-up sign. This is the longest conversation we've ever had, and suddenly Mrs. Welsch seems simultaneously more human to me and more baffling than ever.

To be honest, Mrs. Welsch is kind of freaking me out.

But I don't tell her that. "Great," is what I say instead. "Just leave a comment on the blog about the party, I think."

"You're having a party?" Verbena asks, coming up beside me. "When? Am I invited? What should I wear—costume? Ball gown? Tux?"

"My mom's having a party," I clarify as we head to our usual table. "And everybody in the world is invited, and it doesn't matter what you wear, just as long as you sing along."

It takes me almost the whole lunch period to explain to Verbena what a hootenanny is and why my mom is all fired up about having one.

"It's like this old-fashioned thing," I tell her, "like they used to have in the sixties."

"The 1960s?" Verbena asks, clearly confused.

"No, the 1560s," I reply, exasperated. "Come decked out in your best Christopher Columbus attire."

Verbena leans over and draws a frowny face on my hand with a black Sharpie. "Don't be sarcastic," she admonishes me. "It's just that I've never heard of a hootenjammy—"

"Hootenanny," I correct her, sighing.

"Hoote*nanny*," she says. "And I'm trying to understand. People are going to come over to your house and sing songs? Together?"

"Like one big happy family. With guitars. And, if we're lucky, ukuleles."

Verbena shrugs. "I think it sounds like fun, and your mom sounds like a neat person. Original. My mom never invites anyone over. She gets home from work, throws herself down on the couch, and yells, 'I'm famished, someone go order take-out.' That's why I'm so fat—Chinese take-out and pizza."

"You're not fat," I say. "You're really not. Besides, skinniness is overrated."

"Tall, skinny people always say that," Verbena complains. "You have no idea how hard it is to be five-four. I eat one piece of chocolate, I gain five pounds. By the way, what kind of food is your mom serving at the hoot—uh—hootah-whatever?"

Now we get to the only part of my mom's scheme that doesn't irritate me. "She's having it catered. Allen and

Sons' barbecue, hush puppies, and slaw. The nectar of the gods."

Verbena closes her eyes and gets a dreamy expression on her face. "Mmmm, I love hush puppies, especially when they're just out of the fryer."

"I have a friend who works at Allen and Sons. I bet he'd get you all the hush puppies you wanted."

Allen and Sons is where Monster has a job as a pig smoker and chief hush puppy fryer. "Stop by, I'll hook you up with some 'cue," he told me when he dropped me off at home on Monday. Looking across the table at Verbena, I have a sudden vision of the two of them as a couple. He's big and tall, she's short and curvy, and she probably wouldn't mind that he was big, and I know he wouldn't mind that she was curvy, and they're both—well, unique.

"You want to come with me to Jam Band Friday?" I ask her, thinking I can introduce them and see if any sparks fly. "I could use some friendly support."

"I guess so," Verbena says, popping a sugar-free coffee-flavored toffee into her mouth. "You don't think they play really loud, do you? Really loud music gives me headaches."

Hmmm, maybe Monster and Verbena aren't a match made in heaven after all. Still, you never know.

Jam Band meets at 3:25, right after the last bell Friday afternoon, and I've promised Monster I'll be there. I'm not sure becoming the Jam Band's lone girl bass player is going to help me in my quest for the title of Most Normal High School Student Ever, but at the very least it will up my coolness quotient a good 150 percent.

Friday morning I drop off my bass in the band room. I have to say that one of the coolest moments of my life is walking into school carrying a bass case. One of the uncoolest moments was getting off the bus with it and trying desperately not to injure anyone, but the memory of my embarrassment was totally demolished as I walked by Stonerville, the outside area across from the bus drop-off where all the druggies and wannabe druggies hang out and wish they could smoke cigarettes like the high school stoners of yore.

"Hey, man, she's got a Peavey," a skinny, dreadlocked guy with half-lidded eyes called out, and I heard at least three "awesome's" in reply. I wasn't actually sure what a Peavey was until I looked down at my case and saw that's what was written across the top.

"Are you sure you don't want to come?" I ask Sarah in Great Girls and Women, even though I'm not sure *I* want her to come. Okay, quite frankly, I don't want her to come. Remembering her bored expression while I played over at Monster's, I can't imagine it would be any fun to have Sarah watching me this afternoon. Add that to the fact that Verbena will be there, and who knows what Verbena might say. Something along the lines of *Wow, Sarah, the way Janie describes you, you sound like a huge pain in the butt,* probably.

"No, I'm going over to Whole Foods for a tasting," Sarah says as she shoves her books in her backpack. "The manager says she's got a new line of fair-trade chocolate I'm going to love. We'll see. That last batch they got in from Chile was pretty lame."

"That's awesome," I tell her, trying not to sound too relieved. "Too bad you're going to miss Jeremy play, though."

"Oh, I'm going to watch him play tomorrow night, didn't I mention that?"

I drop my pen. Since when did Sarah make Saturday night plans that didn't include me? "Uh, no. You didn't mention that, as a matter of fact. Where's he playing?"

"Sid's," Sarah says rather nonchalantly, zipping up her backpack. "You know, over at Carr-Mill Mall?"

"I know where Sid's is," I reply testily. "It's my mom's favorite place to eat, remember?"

"Used to be," Sarah corrects me. "Before she turned against it."

Sid's is this great retro diner where we used to go all the time, back before life on the farm. It was the perfect restaurant for Avery, since Avery loves pancakes and Sid's serves pancakes all day long, and back in the old days my mom couldn't make a pancake to save her life. We used to go at least once a week.

"She's against all restaurants now, not just Sid's," I inform Sarah. "They're environmentally incorrect. Like, at Sid's, they bring you water even if you don't ask for it, and a lot of their produce isn't locally grown."

Sarah pretends to be shocked. "Horrors!"

"Yeah, well, you know my mom. So Jeremy's playing at Sid's?"

"At the Saturday night open mic in the back room," Sarah says. She stands up at the sound of the bell. "Emma told me, actually. She's convinced my parents to let her out of the house whenever I need a ride somewhere, and Emma decided I needed a ride to Sid's on Saturday to hang out at the open mic. Some friend of Todd's is playing fiddle in an old-time band."

We walk out the door together, but instead of making a beeline for Jeremy's locker, I turn left to head for the band room, and Sarah heads for the gym.

"See you tomorrow afternoon," I call after her. "You know, to go talk to Mr. Pritchard?"

Sarah doesn't even turn around. "See ya!" she calls out cheerfully, waving a backward hand.

I'm just about to get seriously depressed when Monster appears at my side. "You ready to jam, man? You been practicing?"

I nod. "An hour a day for four straight days," I tell him. "I'm awesome."

"I believe it," Monster says with a grin. "I bet you're a rock-and-roll machine."

I search my brain for a witty reply, but the butterflies in my stomach are distracting me. In five minutes I'm going to be plucking away at a bass guitar in a roomful of strangers, not counting Monster and Verbena. Whose idea was this? Mine? How could it be my idea? I'm not a bass player. I'm not a rock-and-roll machine. I probably won't know any of the songs. Why didn't I ask Monster what songs they play?

My nerves must be showing, because Monster pats me on the back and says, "Don't sweat it, dude. Just a bunch of misfits and malcontents in there. Besides, they'll be too busy trying to show off for you to notice if you don't hit every note."

"Show off for me?"

"Yeah, man, you kidding?" Monster grins. "A cute chick with a bass is a pretty irresistible thing, you gotta admit."

And there it is again, what I've come to think of as the Big Feeling. I don't know what it means or where it comes from.

All I know is at this very minute, I'm feeling it.

I'm the cute chick with a bass.

Now that's a reputation I can live with.

Chapter Fifteen

The Awful Truth About Jeremy Fitch

Jeremy Fitch is happy to see me.

I've been waiting for this moment my entire life.

You know the moment I'm talking about—the "A Cute Boy Smiles at You as You Walk into a Room and He Looks Like He's Really, Really Happy to See You" moment. Even back in fourth grade, when I didn't actually like boys, I still dreamed that one day I'd enter a room—dressed in a fluffy pink ball gown and a sparkling tiara, of course—and cause heads to turn and joy at my presence to abound.

"You finally made it to Jam Band," Jeremy says to me as I head to the back of the room where I've stored my case. "I thought this day would never come."

"Yeah, well—" And once again speech escapes me.

"So what was your name again?"

I'm in the process of pulling my bass out from under a table, but I stop and peer up at Jeremy. I've been stalking him for two months, and he doesn't even know my name? Why do I suddenly feel humiliated beyond belief?

Maybe it's because I'm humiliated beyond belief.

"Yo, Janie!" Monster calls from across the room. "You can share my amp if you didn't bring yours."

I smile gratefully at the one person in this room who actually knows my name. Then Verbena comes in and waves. Now there are two people in the room who know my name.

"Jenny, that's right!" Jeremy says, giving himself a mock slap on the forehead. "How could I forget?"

Two people who know my name, and one who so clearly does not.

"Janie," I tell him, irritation untangling my vocal cords. "Jane-ee. Rhymes with 'rainy.'"

Jeremy grins. "But not with 'Rena.'"

"No, then I would be Gina."

"And that would be bad."

Okay, so he doesn't know my name, but Jeremy Fitch is so cute, I no longer care. The fact is, I've waited a long time for this sort of banter with a boy.

"Very bad," I tell him, smiling. "The worst thing ever."

"Worse than nuclear holocaust," Jeremy agrees.

"Worse than a rock in your shoe," I lob back.

"Come on, Janie, let's get you tuned up," Monster calls to me, and I regretfully say, "Gotta go."

"Come back soon," Jeremy says with a grin.

This guy is dangerously cute.

While Monster tunes the bass, the room fills up with Jam Banders. It's a grab bag of boys, though the balance is leaning toward guys for whom Jam Band is the only place in Manneville High where they fit in. I sense a strong tendency toward black T-shirts with obscure band names and hair that is not tended in any way except for the very occasional shampooing. I see two guys toasting each other with Diet Coke cans and have a sneaking suspicion that Diet Coke is not actually the beverage they're about to partake of. There are a couple of clean-cut albeit cool guys like Jeremy Fitch, guys who don't appear to have a parole officer in their future, but they're in the minority.

I look over at Verbena, who is wiggling her eyebrows at me in mad ecstasy. *We are in Guy Heaven,* her look seems to be saying, or at least in a particular wing of Guy Heaven, the one where everyone says "dude" a lot and regrets that they missed the heyday of Mötley Crüe or else the Germs. This is what I gather from their T-shirts, anyway.

It takes ten minutes for everyone to settle in, get their guitars (it's all guitars, plus one drum kit and my bass) unpacked and tuned up and plugged into their amps. Jam Band is electric, and two seconds into the first song, it is electrifying.

And really, really loud.

Verbena has her fingers in her ears, but she's smiling and bobbing her head. I feel overwhelmed by the noise, but try to keep up. We're playing some old song, something by Radiohead, a song I've never heard before in my life and have no idea how to play, but after about thirty seconds I realize it doesn't matter, because no one can hear me. I close my eyes and have at it. When the song clashes to an end, at least six guys lean toward me and say, "Awesome!"

Monster, sitting next to me, beams with pride.

Verbena claps and bounces up and down. "You were great, Janie!"

My novelty act lasts one more song, and then I settle into being one of the guys. One of the Jam Band guys. We plow through six more songs, interspersed with a lot of arguing about who gets to play lead guitar and what the opening chord is and how the drummer—a kid with a shaved head and Ray-Bans named Pete—is lamer than ever, which causes Pete to throw down his sticks and stalk out of the room.

"He does that every Friday," Monster leans over to inform me. "Fact is, he *is* a lame drummer. We've been trying to get rid of him for two years now. It's a free country, or else we'd lock him out."

I decide I like being part of a group where nobody gets locked out, no matter how lame they are.

At four forty-five, after a particularly raucous rendition of "Whole Lotta Love," Monster stands up and announces, "Gotta pack it in, boys. Janitorial staff locks up at five."

I shrug off my bass. My shoulders are aching, my fingertips are on the verge of blistering, and it's possible I've lost half the hearing in my right ear. Which is why at first I think I've heard wrong when Verbena, caught up in the ecstasy of group participation, jumps up on a desk and announces, "Party at Janie's two weeks from tomorrow, and everybody's invited!"

The room erupts in appreciative whoops. I transmit to Verbena the first harrowing glare of our friendship. Sure, this is just a room of twelve misfit guys and a handful of not so misfits, but party announcements are like viruses. They spread. They get out of control. They end up with the local chapter of Hell's Angels at your front door.

"You still need a ride?" Monster asks me after I put my bass back in its case.

I nod mutely.

"Hey, don't worry about it," Monster tells me, nodding toward Verbena, who is still standing on the desk telling a crowd of Jam Banders that she doesn't actually know where I live, but she'll bring in maps next week. "Half these guys never leave the house. Too busy playing *Guitar Hero*."

There's a tap on my shoulder, and I turn to find Jeremy

Fitch behind me. "Awesome playing today," he tells me. "You're a natural. So you need a ride or something?"

Or something? How about a kiss? A marriage proposal? A trip to Paris? Not necessarily in that order.

"Sure," I respond before I can stop myself. "I'd love—"

That's when I stop myself. "I mean, I've got a ride, but—"

I turn to Monster. "Uh, Jeremy wants to know if I want a ride. I mean, you probably have to go to work or something. . . ."

There is the barest hesitation on Monster's part before he says, "Yeah, as a matter of fact I do, so if you want to catch a ride with the ol' J-Dog, that'd be cool. But how about your friend over there? I can drop her off if she needs a ride."

"Definitely!" I tell him, remembering my plan to bring Monster and Verbena together to see if anything clicks. "She definitely needs a ride."

"Happy to do it," Monster says. "Don't forget to practice this weekend."

"I won't," I promise, clicking shut my case and grinning like a maniac. "At least thirty minutes a day."

Monster gives my shoulder a squeeze. "Attagirl."

And then I follow Jeremy Fitch—*the* Jeremy Fitch—out the door and into the hallway. Two minutes later we're in his car (Honda Civic circa the last millennium) and riding down the road to Farm World. The music pumping out of the Honda's tinny speakers negates the need for small talk, so I relax and look out the window and try not to think about Sarah. Jeremy is just giving me a ride, after all. He hasn't proposed marriage or asked me out on a date—yet. He's just thoughtfully offered me a ride home from school.

I snuggle down into the idea of how wonderfully old-fashioned this feels. An act of honest chivalry, mingled perhaps—a girl can dream—with at least a modicum of romantic interest. Nothing physical will pass between us, of course, not on this ride, but when he drops me off, our eyes will hold for a second longer than necessary and we'll both imagine rides to come. In the meantime, I'm thankful for once that I live way out in the boonies; as far as I'm concerned, the longer it takes to get to my house, the better.

After five minutes of driving, it becomes clear that Jeremy has no idea of just how long this trip is going to take and that it's starting to make him anxious. "Should I turn up here?" he asks, turning the volume down. "Haw River Estates, right?"

"Uh, no." I wave vaguely toward the horizon. "Haw River *Road*. It's about five miles out, off of 15-501."

"But that's Chatham County." Jeremy glances at me, and I can see that he's irritated, as if I'd somehow scammed him into giving me a ride to some faraway land instead of Farm World, which is only a fifteen-minute drive if you don't have to stop for sheep crossings.

"No, it's *almost* Chatham County," I say, trying to keep my tone light. "But we're still in Manneville. I mean, our farm is."

"Your farm? You live on a farm?"

This asked in a tone of voice suggesting I probably also study by firelight and have an extra chromosome or two up my sleeve.

I nod, red-faced, and look miserably out the window. My first chance at love ruined by my Green Acres address. I should have known. I'll never have a boyfriend, because it will be too inconvenient to pick me up on a date and my backyard smells like manure. Any chance of Jeremy Fitch asking me out—blown. Over. Done with.

Just as I'm about to fling myself from the car in despair, it occurs to me that Monster didn't seem to mind the distance when he drove me home on Monday. So what's Prince Charming's deal? It's a beautiful day, and I just had an amazing debut as the Jam Band's bass player. In fact, I kicked some serious Jam Band butt. I sit up straight and turn toward Jeremy, who is tapping impatiently on the steering wheel, as though keeping track of each tenth of a mile we traverse. "Do you have something against farms?" I demand. "A problem with cows? No patience with root vegetables?"

"It's just"—and here his voice goes up a half an octave, like a sixth-grade boy who's lost his milk money—"gas is expensive, man."

This is so uncool. I dig through my backpack and pull out a five. "Will this do?"

(*Please don't take it,* I pray fervently. *Please, please, please.*)

Jeremy takes the bill from me and crams it in his shirt pocket. "Yeah, thanks," he says, leaning over and giving my knee a squeeze. "You're a cool girl. A lot of chicks I know wouldn't understand it costs a lot to fill up a gas tank these days."

Oh, I understand all right. I understand everything I need to understand about Jeremy Fitch.

Just wait until I tell Sarah that Prince Charming isn't such a prince after all.

Chapter Sixteen

Freedom Riders

The backseat of the Bug is cramped with backpacks and various other paraphernalia, but I don't care. Mr. Pritchard sits beside me, his head leaned back, eyes squinting at the sky, a huge smile plastered across his face. Emma has the top down, this being the sort of fall afternoon that requires you breathe in as much fresh air as humanly possible while driving across town in a 1964 VW Beetle convertible with the wind messing up your hair. Mr. Pritchard's hair is white as snow and a little thin, and it's blowing in all sorts of crazy directions, but he doesn't seem to care.

Emma and Sarah ride up front, Emma taking long swigs from a tall paper cup of coffee and glancing every five seconds in the rearview mirror to check out Mr. Pritchard. Over the years, I've known Emma to be quiet, but I've never known her to be dumbstruck. Or starstruck maybe. Clearly she considers Mr. Pritchard a denizen of the upper echelons of Mount Olympus. She even called him "sir" when I introduced them to each other at Pine Manor.

"You just call me Harlan, honey," Mr. Pritchard told her, and Emma's cheeks turned splotchy red, but she shook his hand and said, "Okay, uh, Harlan."

Sarah and I glanced at each other, eyebrows raised. *Uh*? Emma said *uh*?

We're driving across town toward Mrs. Septima Brown's house in Manneville Heights, a rickety subdivision populated by a large percentage of Manneville's African-American senior citizens and home to the BTW Cultural Center, which used to be Booker T. Washington Elementary School, the only black elementary school in Manneville until all the public schools were integrated in the early sixties. For years, busloads of Manneville elementary students, black and white, have made the trek over to the BTW Cultural Center on the Tuesday after the Martin Luther King Jr. holiday to sing "This Little Light of Mine" and watch a film of the "I Have a Dream" speech.

Mrs. Brown's house sits on a lawn so pristine that you have to wonder if she pays someone to stand under the trees on windy days to catch the leaves before they hit the ground. The house itself is tiny, with concrete steps leading up to a porch only big enough for a rocking chair, a small café table, and several potted mums.

Before Mr. Pritchard can ring the bell, the front door

opens and a tall, slightly stooped woman bursts out, a bright orange and red shawl wrapped around her shoulders. She is smiling and moving at approximately a hundred miles per hour.

"Harlan!" she cries, practically leaping into Mr. Pritchard's arms and wrapping him in an enormous hug. "They finally let you out of jail!"

"Only because these fine young ladies agreed to keep an eye on me," Mr. Pritchard replies, waving to where Emma, Sarah, and I wait at the bottom of the steps. "They got rules and regulations over in the pokey, or hadn't you heard?"

Mrs. Septima Brown laughs. "I never was much for jailhouses. I'm somewhat ashamed to admit that now. But I'm glad I've not yet had to retire to the old folks' home."

"Stay away as long as you can," Mr. Pritchard advises. "The smell alone will take years off your life."

Mrs. Brown steps past Mr. Pritchard and perches on the top step. A cool breeze stirs, and she pulls her shawl tightly across her chest. "It certainly is real fall weather we're having here," she says to us, adjusting her glasses as if to see us better. The lenses magnify her dark brown eyes so that they look slightly too large for her head. "And you girls driving around with your car top down! Why don't you come in, and I'll fix you some tea."

We follow Mrs. Brown into her tiny house and take a

seat in her tiny but immaculate living room. There is a distinct lack of grandmotherly clutter—no knickknacks, no lace doilies, no miniature teacups with depictions of the Seven Wonders of the World. Emma squeezes in next to Mr. Pritchard on the scratchy-looking couch, while Sarah sits on a delicate cane-backed chair. I make myself at home on an ottoman near the coffee table. We are only slightly less crammed than we were in the Bug.

"Can I help you with anything?" Emma calls to Mrs. Brown. "I can carry out the tea."

"Oh, no, dear, I have it all here on a tray," Mrs. Brown says, walking back into the living room. "I had everything prepared before you arrived."

With Emma's help, Mrs. Brown passes teacups, then offers around a plate of thin lemon cookies with crisp brown edges. When they finish serving, Mrs. Brown pats Emma on the arm and says, "Thank you for helping, dear. What lovely manners you have."

Emma blushes. Emma, the Queen of Cool, blushes.

It occurs to me that I really don't know her at all.

Mrs. Brown takes a seat in a wingback chair and pulls a brightly colored quilt over her lap. After taking a sip of tea and pronouncing it much too hot to drink, she picks up some knitting from a basket by her feet. "I'm knitting an afghan for an Afghan, my church's latest charity project," she tells us, working the indigo blue yarn with a pair of metallic pink needles. She points to the TV, an old-fashioned model the size of an oven about six inches behind my head. "I watch the History Channel while I knit. It's World War I week. I've decided that to truly understand World War II, you must have all the facts about World War I. And by tonight at ten o'clock, I shall."

We all sit in silence for a minute while Mrs. Brown knits, taking careful sips of our tea. After peering into her cup for what seems like a long time, Emma looks up at Mrs. Brown and says, "I thought you did go to jail."

Mrs. Brown looks at Emma thoughtfully and sets her knitting down on her lap. "Have you been doing research, dear?"

"I Googled you," Emma says. "I mean," she amends when Mrs. Brown looks confused, "I looked you up on the Internet. There was a civil rights site where it said you went to jail with a lot of other literacy teachers, in Mississippi."

"Yes, I did, in the summer of 1964, in Greenville." Mrs. Brown nods. "But only briefly. I allowed myself to be bailed out. Not everyone did. It was a badge of honor to refuse bail. But I just couldn't abide the thought of spending the night in a jailhouse in Mississippi. I was sure we'd be dragged out in the middle of the night and taken somewhere to be shot. I was a coward, really."

"Septima!" Mr. Pritchard exclaims, half rising from his

seat on the couch. "You were no such thing. Why, you're one of the bravest people I know."

Mrs. Brown waves his praise away. "Not at all, Harlan, not at all. I've always sought comfort. It's my great failing, I fear."

Mr. Pritchard harrumphs.

"That really happened to some people," Emma says. "They really did get taken out of jail and killed. It was a reasonable thing to be afraid of."

"I thought so at the time," Mrs. Brown says, returning to her knitting. "But now I see that my friends who spent long stretches of time in jail were practicing what Dr. King would have called 'redemptive suffering.' They were sacrificing themselves bodily for the better of the whole."

Sarah pulls out a small notepad from her back pocket and begins scribbling notes. Suddenly I'm sorry I don't have my dad's recording equipment. Leaning forward, I ask, "Did you get arrested for starting a school? And what is a Citizenship School, exactly?"

A smile lights Mrs. Brown's face. Clearly this is a subject dear to her heart. "Ah, the Freedom School! If only my dear Hazel were here to tell the story with me. But Harlan, you'll help, won't you?"

Mr. Pritchard nods. "I'll do my best."

"Well, you all know where Mason Farm Road is, don't

you?" Mrs. Brown asks, reaching for her cup of tea. "Off of Highway 15?"

"That's where we played youth soccer," Sarah informs her. "Over on the fields there, before you get to the Mason Farm subdivision."

"Did you?" Mrs. Brown sounds delighted. "Then you know where Hazel and I ran our school. There's an old farmhouse there, tucked back behind the creek. . . ."

We all lean forward to listen, Sarah, Emma, and me. Mr. Pritchard leans back and closes his eyes, as if anticipating a treat.

"This is a good story," he says, then reaches over and pats Emma on the knee. "You're going to love this story, just you wait and see. Septima and Hazel did amazing things."

I glance at Emma, and the look on her face does, in fact, look like that of a girl falling in love. Her eyes are wide, her skin is flushed, her mouth is slightly open.

"Now, Harlan," Mrs. Brown says, "you act like you only had a modest part in our school, but you played an important role."

Mr. Pritchard grins. "That's right. I kept the thugs away."

"More than that!" Mrs. Brown protests. She looks at the rest of us. "Starting a school was my idea, but Harlan here's the one who found a place for us to have it. In those days nobody wanted to get the Klan riled up. Oh, it wasn't as bad here as it was in the Deep South, but we had our share of white boys who liked to dress up in robes and ride around like hoodlums. None of the black churches wanted us, not after all those churches were burned in Mississippi. But we had to have some place to hold our reading classes, and it was Harlan who found us our schoolhouse."

"I helped you find an old abandoned farmhouse, if that's what you mean," Mr. Pritchard says. "I'm not sure I was doing you such a great favor. I thought that place might fall in on itself any minute."

"Oh, but we had the best time fixing it up, didn't we?" Mrs. Brown exclaims, leaning forward to take another lemon cookie from the plate on the coffee table. "Like an old-fashioned barn raising. Everybody came! Well, all the black folks came, and a few sympathetic whites, and we got it put back together. And then we started teaching. Hazel loved to teach handwriting, didn't she?"

Mr. Pritchard laughs. "She'd get some kind of mad if someone wanted to use an *X* for their signature. 'Write it out pretty!' she'd tell 'em. Lot of them men, they thought she was crazy, but Hazel thought it was important, if you were going to risk your life registering to vote, that you write your name in a good, strong hand."

"We taught a lot of people to read and write," Mrs. Brown says. "Cletus Miller was ninety-two when he learned to read. As soon as he learned, he marched into the public library and demanded a card. The librarian gave it to him too."

"Mary McConnelly," Mr. Pritchard remembers. "She was on our side."

Sarah stops her scribbling. "How did you and Mrs. Pritchard know each other?"

Mrs. Brown leans back in her chair and closes her eyes for a moment. "Let me see. When did I first meet Hazel? I believe it was when she came to speak at our church."

"About civil rights?" Emma asks.

"About hydrangeas. Hazel often spoke to community groups on horticultural matters. I had a few questions for her afterward, as I'd never had any luck with hydrangeas, and we struck up a gardening friendship. This was around 1955, maybe 1956. It wasn't long after that I had the idea to begin a Citizenship School to help folks learn to read and write so that they could register to vote. As soon as Hazel heard about it, she wanted to help."

"I wish I'd been there," Emma blurts, then blushes furiously. "I mean, I would've liked to help too."

"Yes, I believe you would have," Mrs. Brown says in a soothing voice. "I'm sure you would have been brave enough."

Emma stares at her lap. "Maybe," she says. "I hope so."

Everyone is quiet for a moment. I don't know about

Emma and Sarah, but I'm wondering if I would have been brave enough to help. I think of the burnt cross in Mr. Pritchard's front yard, and I imagine it burning in my yard. I imagine looking out from behind the living room curtains while the Klan stood in my front yard, wanting to teach me a lesson. I imagine flames and gunshots.

I close my eyes. I'm hardly brave enough to *think* about it, much less live it.

"Now, Harlan and Hazel weren't afraid of anything," Mrs. Brown says, breaking the silence. She picks up the teapot and stands to refill our cups. "They acted like nothing or nobody could hurt them."

Mr. Pritchard laughs. "It was you and Hazel who had no fear. I remember driving y'all around to folks' houses at night to get 'em to come to the school. Every time headlights showed up behind us, my blood ran cold. Farther we got out on back roads, the easier it got for someone to take a shot at us without getting caught."

"The hardest thing was getting people to talk to us," Mrs. Brown says, sitting down again. "It was exasperating! I couldn't understand it, until one woman told me she'd lose her job if her employer found out she'd registered to vote."

"Some folks didn't want to admit they couldn't read," Mr. Pritchard adds. "It embarrassed 'em."

Mrs. Brown nods. "Especially the men. It made them

feel like children, not to be able to read or write." She smiles a mischievous grin. "Then Hazel came up with the wonderful idea of paying people to come to school. We got a grant and paid them thirty dollars to come to school two nights a week for three months."

"A lot of folks still stayed home," Mr. Pritchard says. "But we got enough. Of course the first night the school opened, Marshall Logan shot out the windows, which didn't help with student recruitment."

A cold shock runs through me. "Someone shot at you? And you knew who it was?"

"Well, he shouted out a few choice epithets while he was shooting," Mrs. Brown tells us. "Almost everybody in the room recognized his voice, since we all shopped at Logan's Drug up on Franklin Street. So Hazel scooted out to the porch and told him she was going to tell his mother! 'Come back in here! You'll get shot!' we all yelled at her, but she said she'd known that man since he was a baby, and she'd known his mama even longer, and she would not tolerate Marshall Logan shooting at her!"

"He gave us money later," Mr. Pritchard says with a grin. "Helped pay for school supplies."

"His mother made him." Mrs. Brown shakes her head. "Hazel said Mrs. Logan was mortified when she heard that Logan had come after us."

Mrs. Brown and Mr. Pritchard laugh together at this. I

realize they've been laughing the whole time we've been here, that telling this story together has made them happy, even though the work they did was dangerous and hard.

I look at Sarah and Emma, and I know that's what they want someday, to have an amazing story like this to tell, one where they faced obstacles but were brave, one where they made a difference in people's lives.

And that's when I feel the big feeling again—the one I felt the first time I picked up Monster's bass—that strange sense that I'm becoming larger. Just by sitting here listening. Just by understanding how large a person's life can be.

Chapter Seventeen

The Girl with the Lizard Tattoo

I have never been anywhere with Emma Lyman where she didn't spend most of the time reading or else staring moodily into space. Minivan rides to theme parks and history museums, shopping trips to Creekside Mall, and two frozen hours at the Ice Capades every year since Sarah and I were seven, you could always count on Emma's reading and staring. But so far today, I've visited the home of a civil rights hero with Emma and eaten pizza with Emma, and now I'm sitting at Sid's about to hear an old-time fiddle and retro jazz band with Emma, and not once has she pulled out a copy of *Trout Fishing in America* or searched the ceiling for something more interesting than the current company she's with.

We're sitting next to each other in a booth close to the stage waiting for the waitress to bring us some coffee, which Emma seems to consume by the gallon. Across the table, Sarah is writing like a madwoman in her little notebook, holding up a "wait just a sec'" finger to anyone who tries to talk to her. "I've got to copy over my notes from this afternoon," she explains when I ask her what she's doing. "This is amazing stuff, just amazing. Imagine it! Our soccer field was sacred ground, and we had no idea. There ought to be a memorial plaque up or a statue or something."

Then a feral look enters her eyes, and there can be no doubt that Sarah is going to be standing in front of the town council at its next meeting, demanding that a statue of Septima Brown and Hazel Pritchard be erected in the middle of the Mason Farm Road soccer fields *pronto*. As in *now*.

"So you and Monster," Emma says when Sarah returns to her feverish scribbling. "You're a thing?"

I look over at her, surprised at the sheer, well, high schooliness of this question. We spent two hours this afternoon with a woman who not only was on a first-name basis with Martin Luther King Jr., but actually chastised him for not putting more women in leadership positions. We have been riding around in a VW Bug with a man who got members of the Klan locked up behind bars at a time when hardly anyone was convicted of crimes against blacks.

All afternoon we'd listened to stories of people walking three miles at night to get to the school, eighty-year-old men writing their names for the first time in their lives, and people getting shot at but still coming just so they could have the right to vote.

And now Emma wants to discuss my love life?

Emma shrugs, as if she's read my thoughts. "Maybe it's trivial, but I just happen to think you and Monster make an interesting pair. I mean, you're basically young and unformed, and yet you have the good sense to hang out with Monster Monroe. I never would have predicted it, to be honest."

I frown, feeling slightly offended. "You don't think I'm good enough for Monster?"

"I'm not sure you're cool enough for Monster," Emma says matter-of-factly, taking the cup of coffee our waitress holds out to her. "Though after today, I'm reconsidering that opinion. I mean, those boots seriously rock. You always did have good clothes, though. Very original."

I stick a purple-cowboy-booted foot into the aisle for all to admire. "I bought these on Zappos.com," I tell her. "And Monster and I are just friends."

"You're an idiot then," Emma says, pouring cream into her coffee. I wait for further commentary, but she appears to have lost interest in me.

I'm saved having to contemplate my idiocy in solitude by the entrance of Todd the Biker, who slides into the booth next to Sarah.

"Hey, little sister," he greets her, then reaches across the table and chucks Emma under the chin. It seems like something you might do to a two-year-old, especially when Emma bites Todd's finger in response.

"I'm Sarah," Sarah says, offering her hand to Todd. "We've met."

Todd dislodges his finger from Emma's incisors and shakes Sarah's hand. "On several occasions. Or at least once." He turns back to Emma. "Hey, babe, sorry I'm late."

Todd and Emma proceed to have a very adult-sounding conversation about Todd's long day at work. The phrase "like an old married couple" springs to mind. I have to say that wild child Emma has not been living up to her billing today.

As the first act—a trio of guitar players in overalls and feedlot baseball caps—tunes up on stage, Todd asks to switch seats with me. He asks politely, almost gallantly, in fact. Up close, he's not as scary-looking as he is when perched on his bike—his hog?—dressed from head to toe in black leather. He has a square jaw and gentle blue eyes, and is, in fact, quite hunky, I see now that I get a chance to truly eyeball him.

As he slips in next to Emma, he pulls a copy of *The Four Quartets* by T. S. Eliot out of his back pocket and puts it on the table. "You're going to have to explain that whole time present/time past thing to me, babe," he says, giving

Emma a kiss on the cheek. "It's twisting my brain around."

Consider my brain twisted as well.

Sarah finishes her notes with a flourish, then looks around and asks, "Why hasn't the waitress been by yet? I need some coffee, and I need it now."

"She's been by three times," I inform her. "I think she's given up on you."

"Maybe she'll give me another chance," Sarah says, and waves down our server, who has the sort of bleached-blond crew cut I wish I had the nerve to try and a tattooed lizard peeking out over the neck of her T-shirt.

Sarah raises her eyebrow at me, nodding almost imperceptibly toward the lizard. One of our inviolable agreements is that neither of us will ever get a tattoo. We believe strongly in funkiness, in great shoes, fabulous clothes, and excellent, preferably vintage, accessories, but tattoos reek of trying too hard to be cool.

Authentic funkiness means never trying too hard.

I feel good, back here in the land where Sarah and I are friends and have understandings and inviolable agreements. In fact, I feel so good, I decide it's time to share the bad news about Jeremy Fitch. He's unromantic, a cheapskate, and—if we want to be totally honest here—not that great of a guitar player. I noticed yesterday at Jam Band that he lost his place in songs a lot and sometimes was fake-strumming instead of actually playing along.

"So I never told you about Jam Band," I begin, and Sarah scootches a little closer to me, smiling, ready to hear some great Jeremy Fitch story. But just as I'm about to break the bad news to her that the Jeremy who has lived all fall in our imaginations doesn't actually exist, the real, live version appears.

"I can't believe you're here!" Jeremy stands beside our table and grins his big, charming grin, brushing his hand through his bangs to get them out of his eyes. "Awesome!"

I can feel Sarah staring—at me. Which may have something to do with the fact that I'm the one Jeremy appears to be directing his comments to.

"Yeah, we're here," I stammer. "The whole gang." I lean toward Sarah, wishing like anything that Jeremy would acknowledge her.

"Hey, Cheryl," Jeremy says, picking up on my cue. "Glad you could make it."

"It's Sarah."

Says Emma.

Sarah and I whip our heads around. Emma is glaring at Jeremy. "Why can't you ever get anybody's name right? Ever since eighth grade, you've been calling girls by the wrong name. It's like some bizarre power play."

"I know your name, Emma," Jeremy says. He's smiling, but there's something unpleasant beneath it. "How could I ever forget it?"

"Man, I hate charming guys," Emma mutters. She turns to Todd. "Don't get me wrong, babe. You definitely have your charms. You just don't wield them like a weapon."

"I'm uncomfortable with weapons," Todd admits, wrapping a large hand around his coffee mug. "With violence in general, actually."

Emma gives his arm an affectionate squeeze. "'Nonviolence is a weapon of the strong,' babe."

"Man, I love Gandhi!" Todd exclaims. "Except for that diaper thing he wore. That kind of freaks me out."

Jeremy leans down so that we're face-to-face. "Come find me after our set. I want to hear what you think."

"What was that about, Janie?" Emma wants to know as we all watch Jeremy walk off in the direction of the kitchen. "You're not—? I mean, you couldn't possibly—?" She turns toward Sarah. "Tell me Janie doesn't have a thing with Jeremy Fitch."

"How should I know?" Sarah has pulled herself into a small, miserable ball in the corner of the booth. "Janie seems to be very socially active these days."

"You know I don't," I tell her. "In fact, I think he's a creep. He made me pay for gas."

Emma raises an eyebrow. "He made you pay for gas? Do tell."

"Yesterday, after Jam Band. He offered me a ride home, but when he realized how far out I lived, he sort of implied that I should chip in for gas. I offered him five dollars, but I didn't think he'd take it."

"That doesn't mean anything," Sarah insists. "I mean, you should have offered to pay anyway, right? Unless you thought you guys were on some sort of date. Is that what you thought?"

"Hey, Cinderella," Emma says, leaning over to tap Sarah on the wrist. "It's the last stroke of midnight, come back to Realityville."

Sarah jerks her hand back. "What do you mean by that?"

"Jeremy Fitch is lame, okay? He lives to flirt, hates to commit. The more girls in love with him the better. And, hey, he's cute, I admit it, but life's too short. You guys deserve somebody better, somebody with some substance. Somebody like Todd."

Todd waves his copy of *The Four Quartets* at us. "I'm a keeper," he says with a goofy grin.

Then Emma looks across the room and her face lights up. She turns to me. "You deserve someone like Monster Monroe," she tells me, pointing at the doorway.

And there he is, Monster, tall and broad-shouldered, bass in hand, fielding greetings from all over Sid's.

And there's Verbena, right behind him.

Chapter Eighteen

Night of the Living Accordions

Verbena squeals when she sees me.

She is the first squealing friend of my friendship career.

"I can't believe I'm actually doing something on a Saturday night!" she calls as she rushes over to our table. "Monster gave me a ride. Well, he's the one who told me about the open mic in the first place, and then I *begged* him for a ride. We talked about you the whole way over! I mean, how great and cool you are and everything."

I have about thirty-seven different thoughts and impressions rushing around my brain all at once. I have the impression, for instance, that Sarah is staring at Verbena openmouthed, as though she has just been shot with a stun gun. I have the thought that Emma might find Verbena a little bit, well, verbose, for one thing and quite possibly vapid, for another, but any negative vibes from Emma are overridden by my sense that Todd finds my cherubic and very enthusiastic friend delightful beyond measure.

But the thought hovering over all other thoughts, the thought I find quite disturbing and am exerting a great deal of effort not to think, is this one: I am overwhelmingly relieved that Verbena is not here as Monster's date.

Not that Monster is my type.

The band onstage launches into its first song, an original ditty entitled "Tears for Tina" about—get this—love gone wrong, and any possibility of further conversation is put to rest. Verbena squeezes into the booth next to me and begins keeping time with my coffee spoon. At one point she leans sideways and yells into my ear, "I feel like I've finally arrived!"

I glance over at Sarah, whose expression seems to say, *And now why don't you go away?*

I want to reach out to her somehow, give her a little shoulder bump (Sarah's not big on emotional displays, but the occasional shoulder bump's okay) or a sympathetic smile. Because suddenly there's something about Sarah that strikes me as sad. Not sad as in *pathetic*, but sad as in . . . I don't know, lost, I guess. Which seems a funny thing to say about a girl who has firm career plans, is waging an impressive campaign against child slave labor in the cocoa fields of the Ivory Coast, and is at this very minute planning a multimillion-dollar civic project to honor two of our community's civil rights heroes.

But in spite of all that, it occurs to me that I'm not the only one who's spent this fall feeling unconnected, uncertain, and a little bit lonely.

The first band is quickly followed by a girl folk singer whose long, copper-colored hair swings in a beautiful arc in front of her face as she whines out songs about—you'll never believe it—love gone wrong. Several of Folk Singer Girl's bad love songs end with mutilated corpses, which draws a posse of black T-shirted guys close to the stage to cheer her on.

We sit through two more acts before Jeremy's band comes up. To my surprise, Monster is playing bass. I don't know why I'm surprised. He and Jeremy are friends, after all, and Monster did show up here with bass in hand. I realize that in the short history of our friendship, I've never heard Monster play anything but guitar.

Tonight he's shed of his overalls, and his hair hangs free from its usual ponytail. Monster's wearing faded black jeans, Doc Martens, and a T-shirt that reads—I choke on my coffee when I see this—REDNECKS FOR PEACE.

"What is it with you and choking?" Verbena asks, pounding me on the back. "Close up that windpipe when you swallow!"

I nod at this sound piece of advice and turn back to the stage. Monster's bass anchors every song, and after my short but deep immersion into the world of bass playing,

I can testify to the fact that he's good. He rocks back and forth while he plays, one long leg extended behind him, the other bent in front of him. It has the effect of making Monster look like a tree being blown around in a hurricane. A tree with roots that go way down.

Every eye in the audience is on him. No one can help it. There is something incredibly compelling about a six-foot-two guy who is walking a tightrope between exquisite control and unleashed power. I wonder what would happen if he suddenly came uprooted, if his rocking threw him forward into the audience or back against the brick wall behind him. Mayhem, either way. That's where the thrill of watching him comes in, I realize—the possibility of danger.

Next to Monster, Jeremy Fitch looks cute and boyish and entirely beside the point. He's doing an okay job of playing, and he's not a bad singer, but he doesn't have Monster's presence. I glance over at Sarah, who shrugs at me. It's hard to know if she's ready to let Jeremy—the *idea* of Jeremy—go or not.

When the set is over, Verbena is on her feet and dragging me out of the booth. "Come on, Janie! Let's go tell Monster how awesome he is!"

I turn to Sarah. "You want to go say something to Jeremy? He was good up there."

Sarah shakes her head. "I don't actually know him that well," she says. This from the girl who's been studying

Jeremy Fitch nonstop for the last two months. "Besides, I think you're the one he's interested in seeing."

"He doesn't even know my name," I tell her. "Anyway, I bet Monster would appreciate you coming over to say hi. And Jeremy probably would too."

Emma looks across the table at her sister. "Did you like the set?"

Sarah nods.

"Me too. So let's all go up and say, 'Great set, we want to be your groupies.'"

Sarah reluctantly slides out of the booth.

There's a crowd around Monster, Jeremy, and the other two guys in their band. The girls are clamoring around Jeremy, while a bunch of guys surround Monster with a chorus of "Awesome, dude!" When Monster sees our little contingent, he breaks out in a huge grin.

"What'd y'all think?" he calls over. "Good show or what?"

I can't help it. "Awesome, dude!" I call back.

Monster breaks through his fan club to come over to where we're standing. He points a finger at me. "You're going to be up there one day soon."

"By myself? Solo bass?"

"Yeah, dude! It's been done."

I feel a pinch of disappointment when Monster calls me dude.

Not that he's my type.

Then Monster turns to Sarah. "I been thinking about you. You know what might be perfect? An accordion." He holds up a hand when Sarah begins to protest. "An accordion's gonna hit right at your center of gravity, you being on the short side."

"And just who am I going to play accordion with?" Sarah wants to know, sounding highly skeptical. "Is the circus in town?"

Monster looks at Emma. "How 'bout it, Em? Everybody's got a thing for a sister act."

Emma looks like she's trying to decide just how crazy this idea is. Her expression suggests: pretty freakin' crazy.

But then Todd leans over and puts a gentle hand on her shoulder. "Klezmer music, babe. Think about it. You'd be a natural."

Emma's expression brightens. "Klezmer music," she says dreamily. "I love klezmer music."

Todd gives her a nudge. "Huh? Huh? I think you know what I'm saying."

"You want to start a klezmer band?" Emma asks, turning to Sarah, still not sounding 100 percent sure that this is a good idea. "Could be fun."

"Klezmer band?" Sarah looks at her sister as though questioning her sanity. At the same time, there's a little glimmer in her eye. An Emma opportunity! "I don't even know what that is."

I take a step back. Not only does Sarah not know something, she has just freely admitted it.

Change is definitely in the air.

"Klezmer is Jewish folk music," Emma explains, sounding like the Lyman sisters performing in a Jewish folk music band is the most natural thing in the world.

"But we're not Jewish," Sarah points out. "We're Catholic."

"So what? There's no rule that you have to be Jewish."

Todd stands behind Emma and rubs her shoulders. "'I am large, I contain multitudes.'"

Emma twists around and gives Todd a glowing smile. "Whitman." She sighs. "He gets everything right."

"Hey!" Verbena exclaims. "If it's folk music, you guys could play at Janie's mom's hooten-athingy!"

"Excellent!" Emma exclaims, as though needing no further explanation of what a hooten-athingy is. She gestures enthusiastically at Sarah. "Monster, let's get this girl an accordion, and one for me, too."

"I know a guy who can hook me up," Monster says. "Anybody else need one?"

Todd, Verbena, and I all politely decline.

Back at our table, waiting for Todd's friend's old-time fiddle and vintage jazz band to start its set, we order another round of coffee. When it arrives, Emma holds up her mug. "To Mrs. Septima Brown and Mr. and Mrs. Harlan Pritchard," she toasts. "Knights of the Realm."

"Hear, hear," we chorus, even Verbena, who has no idea what Emma is talking about.

Todd puts an affectionate arm around Emma. "To us," he toasts her, and then he looks around the table. "Live large."

"Live large," we say, lifting our mugs, and then I bump Sarah's shoulder with mine, and she doesn't even get mad when coffee spills onto her lap.

"Hear, hear," she says. And then again, whispering, "Hear, hear."

Chapter Nineteen

How to Make an American Quilt

Like Todd, I am a nonviolent person. I come from a nonviolent family. My dad keeps an ax in the barn to kill snakes with, but that's the only weaponry I know of on the premises.

But when Ty Cobb wakes me up at 6:52 a.m. on Sunday morning, it crosses my mind that if I had a loaded shotgun under my bed, we could be eating rooster for breakfast.

Just a thought.

It doesn't help that I didn't fall asleep until after three. Emma dropped me off around eleven thirty last night, but I couldn't get my brain to settle down. Okay, so maybe drinking four cups of coffee at Sid's wasn't the greatest idea in the world, but even if I'd been downing decaf, I still would have had problems dozing off. If you start your day with talk about Freedom Schools and end it with the promise of klezmer music to come, it's just plain hard to sleep.

I snuggle deeper under my quilt in hopes that there's a hungry copperhead in the yard that will make Ty Cobb a thing of the past, but no such luck.

"All right, you stupid rooster," I yell in the direction of the closed window. "I'm up already!"

I struggle out of bed and down the stairs. Avery is at the kitchen table, reading the Sunday comics to my mom, who's at the stove making spinach and goat cheese frittatas and pretending to pay attention. "Oh, that's funny!" she says at odd intervals, causing Avery to roll her eyes and say, "Mom, it's not the funny part yet."

"Janie!" my mom calls out when she sees me. "I have a great idea for how to spend the afternoon!"

"Mom, it's not even seven." I plop into my chair at the table, almost missing it. "Why are we talking about the afternoon?"

"Does the phrase 'quilting bee' mean anything to you?" she asks, ignoring my query and crumbling some cheese into the pan of eggs she's got cooking. "Because they're having one over at White Pine Methodist Church, just down the road. Everyone's invited!"

"Mom, you don't know how to quilt," I remind her. "You barely know how to sew."

"I'm getting better," my mom insists. She points to the

apron tied around her waist. "I made this, didn't I?"

The apron is a hemmed square of pink calico fabric with ties that are barely hanging on. Uneven stitches and loose threads abound. It's an apron in quotes, a rag in the making.

I nod in agreement. "Yes, you did, Mom. I think that's my point."

My mom gives me a hurt look. "Maybe I don't have your sewing talent, but I'm getting better. It'll just take practice, that's all."

Now I feel guilty. "No, no, you're right. And I like your apron. The fabric is really nice."

My mom's face brightens. "So you'll go with me? To the quilting bee? Avery's coming too."

Avery beams at me from over the newspaper. "Please come, Janie? It'll be so much fun!"

I sigh. "Do I have a choice?"

And much to my surprise, it's my dad who says, "No, you don't."

"Mike?" My mom looks at my dad, who's standing in the kitchen doorway. We all do. My dad is a champion of staying out of things, which includes keeping his opinions on mother-daughter conflicts to himself.

"I think it's time Janie rejoined the family," my dad says. "I'm tired of her acting like we're not good enough for her anymore."

I feel like I've been slapped. "I don't think I'm too good for you," I stammer out after a minute. "I just—I—"

"She's fourteen, for Pete's sake," my mom says to my dad. "Don't you know anything about fourteen-year-old girls?"

"Not much," my dad admits. "But I don't think being fourteen excuses you from having a nice word for your mother from time to time."

My mom laughs and waves a dish towel at him, like he's a pesky fly she's trying to get out of her kitchen. "That won't happen again until she's fifteen, honey." Then she turns to me. "You don't have to come to the quilting bee with us, Janie. I just thought since you're so interested in sewing, it might be fun for you."

"I'll go," I say in a quiet voice.

"Well, wonderful," my mom replies. "Now let me get you something to eat."

After breakfast, I take care of the goats and then go back to bed until eleven. I've just gotten out of the shower and am standing in front of my closet wrapped in a towel, wondering what one wears to a quilting bee, when Avery comes to my door carrying my cell.

"I answered it for you," she tells me, and then, before I have a chance to blow up at her, she says in a loud whisper, "It's a boy! And when I told Daddy his name is Monster, Daddy said I should stand outside your door and eavesdrop because he didn't like the sound of that name, but Mommy said I should give you your privacy."

I take the phone. "Did you hear all of that?" I say into the receiver.

"I've got it all written down," Monster replies. "Your mom sounds cool."

"How about my dad?"

"He sounds like a dad."

We share a moment of silence in honor of the uncoolness of overprotective dads everywhere, or maybe because I can't think of anything else to say. I am suddenly supremely aware of the fact that I'm only wearing a towel, a fact I don't share with Monster.

"Anyway, I don't think I ever got a chance to tell you that you played great on Friday. You got a natural sense of rhythm, which is essential if you're really gonna play bass right. I mean right, like Cliff Burton right or Bootsy Collins right. Even Mike Watt right, if you're into the L.A. punk thing."

"I don't know much about it—the L.A. punk thing, I mean." I pause. "Or anything else you just said."

"You want a mix tape?" Monster offers. "I'll do a showcase mix, introduce you to a wider spectrum of excellent bass playing."

Rivulets of cold water are parading down my neck and back. "Sure," I say, hiking up my towel. "That would be great."

"Anyway," Monster says, "I thought you might want to do some practicing this afternoon."

"I'd like to, but I can't," I tell him. "I'm going to a quilting bee with my mom. Don't ask me why."

"Over at White Pine?"

I hold the receiver away from my ear and look at it. How does Monster know? Is he a quilting aficionado, or just psychic?

"That's where my granny goes to church," he says. "She's crazy about quilts. Crazy about church. Used to make me go every Sunday. The amazing thing, given the nature of my family, is that she herself ain't crazy. Well, maybe halfway crazy, but then everybody's about halfway crazy."

"Well, I'll look for her there," I say, pulling a flannel shirt from my closet in hopes of putting some clothes on soon. "Does she resemble you in any way?"

"She's the spitting image."

"Red hair?"

"And six feet tall. She's a bruiser, Granny."

"She sounds sort of scary," I say, plopping down on my bed and pulling the flannel shirt around my shoulders.

"Least scary person in the world, in spite of her girth," Monster assures me. "Tell her you know me, she'll give you the shirt off her back."

Which, thinking about it after we hang up, sounds exactly

like Monster Monroe himself. The same Monster Monroe who just called me, I realize. On a Sunday morning. To ask me to do something.

How do you feel about this, Janie Gorman? the interviewer asks, sticking a microphone in my face.

No comment, I reply.

Monster's grandmother is the first person I see when we walk into the meeting room at White Pine Methodist. You can't miss her. Most of the women sitting around the huge quilting frame are your typical little old ladies, white haired and shrunken, with Kleenex at the ready. Monster's grandmother looks like she just wandered in off a football field somewhere.

"Hey, girls!" she calls out in a surprisingly high voice when she sees us standing in the doorway. "Y'all come for the quilting? Just pull up a seat and fit yourselves in."

"I've mostly come to watch and learn," my mom tells her. "Now, Janie here"—she puts her hands on my shoulders and pushes me forward a few feet—"she's a wonderful seamstress, though she hasn't done much quilting."

Monster's grandmother waves me over. "Well, you come sit right here next to me, honey. My name is Trena. I'll show you how to use a quilting needle. You just got to learn to rock it like a baby, that's all."

"I know Monster," I say, pulling a chair in next to hers. "He's a friend of mine at school."

Trena smiles and pats her heart with a delicate, if rather large, hand. "Oh, my Monster! Well, I call him Monny, don't you know, because Monster is a ridiculous name, but typical of that mama and daddy of his. His daddy being my son, Emmett, but he's a long story and not one you can tell right next to a church sanctuary, no sir."

Then Trena proceeds to tell me everything about Monster's family, interspersing her tale of woe with quilting hints. "Ed—that's my dearly departed husband—and me, we done everything we could to raise that boy right (you got to rock that needle, honey, just poke it right through the fabric and then kinda work it back and forth just a little bit—now don't worry, you ain't gonna hurt nothing, unless you poke your own finger), and he was fine till he turned sixteen and went girl crazy on us (now pull that thread taut, but don't pucker up the material, if you know what I mean). Started a-drinking and smoking that pot, oh, Lord, it 'bout nearly killed me."

"Did he ever get in trouble?" I ask, not wanting to be too nosy, but curious all the same. "Like go to jail?"

"Oh, Lord, no, child, it never got that bad. He's just no-account is all, and Monny's mama is the same way. How they brung up a boy as good as Monny, I don't know. Well, he stayed with me most of the time, but now I'm at the nursing home, due to failing health, and there's no place for Monny to stay."

"You look healthy to me," I say. "Extremely healthy."

"It's the diabetes, don't you know, so now I got kidney damage. They got me on dialysis twice a week."

Across the table, my mom is quizzing a woman with blue hair on quilting patterns and techniques. Avery is sitting in the lap of a frail-looking octogenarian, who is helping her guide her needle in and out of the fabric.

"You got a nice family, I can tell just by looking at 'em," Trena says. "It's no wonder you turned out so nice yourself. It's folks like Monny who're the mysteries. I think he just must have been born with a good heart."

"He's a very nice person," I agree.

"He surely is." Trena glances up from her sewing. "Any girl would be lucky to have him."

"I hear that a lot," I tell her, keeping my eyes on my work.

We sew in silence for a few minutes. From across the quilting frame I can sense my mom's happiness at being part of such a homemade, authentic event. This will be on the blog tomorrow, count on it. In fact, two seconds after I have this thought, my mom whips out her digital camera and asks, "May I?"

"Oh, honey, I look a sight," someone says, and someone else says, "If I'd known folks were taking pictures, I would've worn something other than these rags," and everyone else says pretty much the same thing, but all over the room hands are patting down hair and lipsticks are being plucked from purses. My mom happily snaps photos of the women demonstrating complicated stitches as they smile big, waxy Ravishing Red smiles.

"I like your mama," Trena tells me. "She seems like good people."

"Smile!" my mom calls to me from across the room, and I look at her and smile. Because she is good people. And she means well, even if she does drive me crazy.

Besides, she makes a mean spinach and goat cheese frittata.

Chapter Twenty

The Good Old Boy Blues

When I walk into the library on Monday afternoon, Verbena is sitting at our usual table, but she has company, a boy I recognize from Friday's Jam Band session. Jason somebody. I notice that Verbena hasn't unpacked her purse snacks, hasn't pulled her journal from her backpack.

"Jason and I are headed for the cafeteria," she says when I reach the table. "You want to come?"

"It's sloppy joe day," Jason informs me. "You don't want to miss that."

I drop my pack on the table and ponder. Lunch in the cafeteria? After all these months—well, all two and a half of them—of social seclusion? Lunch with at least two other people, presumably spent chatting away over our yellow trays, ducking the napkins and empty milk cartons being lobbed from one jock table to another? Maybe waving at a friend walking past, yelling out a joke to a passing acquaintance?

"I've already eaten at my locker," I say finally. "I'd look stupid just sitting there."

"I'm serious, man, the sloppy joes are exponentially good," Jason insists. "If you don't have any money, I'll buy one for you. You can pay me back at your earliest convenience."

Wow, talk about your offers impossible to refuse.

Even before we walk in the door, a feeling of post-traumatic-stress-syndrome panic hits me. I flash back to those early days of lunch in the cafeteria, me eating alone at one of the small, round loser tables, the only kids making eye contact clearly those who had witnessed some aspect of the amazing Farm Girl. A smirk meant they'd seen me on Hay Head Day; an exaggerated scratching of the calf meant they'd seen the worm castings rash in PE.

That's all in the past, I tell myself as I follow Verbena and Jason through the sloppy joe line. How many dramas and embarrassments have taken the place of mine in the collective memory of Manneville High since then? Hundreds of broken zippers and visible bra straps, numerous incidents of public flatulence, teeth plagued by spinach, breath overwhelmed by nasty-smelling bacteria, stupid answers to easy questions, public declarations of love met with icy silences. I'd had a few unfortunate situations early in the semester. Who would even remember?

We carry our trays to a table in the middle of the cafeteria, neither prominently located nor tucked away from the fray. After I'm done eating my sloppy joe—which was, just as Jason promised, remarkably tasty—I lean back in my chair and look around. Now that I'm sitting in the cafeteria with friends, happily blended in, it doesn't look like such an intimidating place. Okay, I wouldn't set my tray down at the cheerleaders' table without an engraved invitation, and the kids in the chains and leather won't be getting an unsolicited hug from yours truly any time soon, but other than that, it's not so scary.

I see Stoner Guy No. 1 from the bus walking in the direction of our table and I smile. Sure, he was part of one of the most humiliating moments of my high school career, but hey, he's a stoner, he'll never remember when—

"Yo, Skunk Girl, you smelling up the joint today or what?"

A few people at nearby tables turn to look at me. *Skunk Girl*, somebody repeats, and there are a few stupid twitters in response.

"I mean, dude, that was some nasty stuff on your shoe," Stoner Guy No. 1 says, coming closer. "Goat, right? Price you pay for living on a farm, I guess." He starts strumming an air guitar and sings, "'They all asked about you, down on the farm, the cows asked, the pigs asked, the horses asked too.'"

He looks up at me and grins. "Little Feat, dude. Anyway, Skunk Girl, you don't smell so bad today, but man, I'll tell you, that morning—whew!"

Now even more people are looking at us, and some are calling out questions to Stoner Guy No. 1, asking if I'd been sprayed by a skunk or just smelled like a skunk naturally.

"Could we get out of here?" I plead with Verbena and Jason. "I don't know how much more of this I can take."

"I've got a beer in my backpack," Jason tells me sympathetically. "Wanna go drink it? 'Cause you look like you could use a beer right about now."

I nod. The first day of school, if you'd told me I'd be the kind of girl who drank beer on school property, I would have laughed in your face. Not the future president of the student council, no way.

Now it seems like the only sensible thing to do.

But just as I'm about to get out of my seat, I think of Cletus Miller, the Freedom School student who didn't learn to write his name until he was ninety-two. Imagine that, sitting down at a desk at the age of ninety-two and being taught the alphabet. Imagine sounding out the letters—*C* as in cat, *L* as in lemon—and painstakingly writing them down in your notebook.

I wonder what sort of names Cletus Miller got called when he went to register to vote. Probably something a lot worse than Skunk Girl. Whatever they called him, I bet Cletus Miller ignored them and just kept on writing his name.

I think it's safe to say what I've had to put up with in ninth grade pales in comparison to Cletus Miller.

"Hey, Stoner Guy!" I yell out, and Stoner Guy No. 1 breaks off comparing the smell of goat manure to that of dog crap and looks at me. "Give peace a chance, why don't you?" I say in my politest, most nonviolent voice.

His mouth drops open. "Huh?"

"Shut up," I clarify.

"Dude," he says. "That hurts."

"Still want that beer?" Jason asks as we watch Stoner Guy No. 1 make his way to the exit.

"I'm good," I tell him. "But I wouldn't mind another sloppy joe."

I'm about to carry my tray back to the food line when I see Mrs. Welsch standing at the cafeteria entrance, looking a little lost. Has the absence of her two most loyal lunchtime customers unnerved her? Sure enough, when she sees me she waves and looks relieved.

"Janie! Your dad just called, honey," she says, coming toward me. "Well, he called the office, actually, and someone told the secretary you were probably in the library, so they came and told me, and I knew you were here. You need to call him back, okay?"

"What's wrong?" I stammer, putting my tray down on an empty table.

Mrs. Welsch consults the piece of paper in her hand. "He says to tell you it's not an emergency, but he did have something he wanted to tell you. And here's his cell phone number, in case you don't know it by heart." She hands the paper to me. "You can use the phone in my office. No cells in school, dear."

Mrs. Welsch's office is at the back of the library. Stacks of books are everywhere and the floor is littered with copies of *Publishers Weekly* and *School Library Journal* bookmarked with yellow sticky notes. "I'll just clear a path for you," Mrs. Welsch tells me, scooping up magazines. "After last spring's budget cuts, I don't have an assistant anymore, and the student intern they gave me this semester is, well"—she looks at me with a pained expression—"not at all interested in books *or* keeping things in order around here."

Then she pushes a pile of papers to the side of the desk and offers me a seat. "Just punch nine for an outside line," she says. "Now I'll give you some privacy."

When my dad answers, the first thing he does is assure me that nothing has happened to my mom or Avery.

"Is it one of the goats?" I ask. "Nothing happened to Loretta Lynn, did it? I was worried about her this morning; it seemed like she was sort of sluggish, and she didn't give much milk—"

My dad interrupts me. "It's Mr. Pritchard, honey. He, well, he, uh—passed last night. Passed away. In his sleep. They called me from the nursing home around nine this morning to let me know, and the woman I talked to said he spent all day yesterday going on and on about what a wonderful time he'd had with you girls and visiting with Mrs. Brown. She said she hadn't seen him so happy in a long time. Anyway, I just thought it was important to let you know."

"Uh, okay," I say, unable to think of anything more substantial to say.

My dad seems to understand. "I'm sure it's a shock, since you just saw him Saturday. But, you know, he was a pretty old guy. Eighty-nine, and he'd known for a while he was close to the end. He had a great life, and with any luck, he's running around in some other dimension with Hazel as we speak."

When I get off the phone, I search around in my backpack for the picture I drew of Mr. Pritchard in his front yard, Mrs. Pritchard peeking around the corner of the house.

It cheers me up.

A little.

I need to tell Sarah and Emma, I realize. It will matter to them—a lot—that Mr. Pritchard died, even though they only knew him for one day. I stand up to leave, and all of a sudden I feel sort of shaky, like my knees aren't working quite right. I guess the fact that Mr. Pritchard died matters a lot to me, too.

I walk down the hallway toward Sarah's locker, feeling sadder by the step. Sad because Mr. Pritchard's dead, and sad that I was born too late to help him and Mrs. Pritchard and Mrs. Brown with their school. Sad that I'm fourteen and I can't figure out how to live large. Sad because I will never be as courageous and amazing as they were.

By the time I reach Sarah's locker, I'm pretty convinced that my life has no meaning at all.

Sarah, on the other hand, is jumping up and down like life is not only meaningful, but also quite fabulous. "You'll never believe it, but Monster has already gotten accordions for me and Emma! He brought them over last night, along with some books on how to play them, and we've already learned 'How Much Is That Doggie in the Window?'!"

Then she pauses and looks at me. "Wow, you look seriously bummed. What's wrong?"

So I tell her about Mr. Pritchard, and she slumps against her locker. "He was such a nice man," she says, tearing up. "I'm not sure if we should tell Emma, though. In fact, that might be an awful idea."

"We have to tell her," I insist. "She'd find out anyway."

Sarah sighs. "I know. But she was working up this

scheme for Mr. Pritchard to come live with us, and she even had my mom halfway convinced that it was a good idea."

"Really? Don't you think Mr. Pritchard would have been sort of radical for your parents?"

"My parents are more fiscal conservatives than social conservatives," Sarah says, grabbing her math book from her locker and slamming the door shut. "They're actually pretty progressive on social issues. Well, except for premarital sex. And drug usage. And boy-girl sleepovers."

We find Emma in the art room, twisting wire into a cage. Beside her on the table is a trio of shorn Barbies wearing prison uniforms. "I'm making a statement," she tells us when she sees us in the doorway.

"What kind of statement?" I ask.

Emma shrugs. "I haven't decided yet. All I know is if I want an A, I'd better make a statement."

Sarah picks up a Barbie and examines it. "Is this one of my old Barbies?"

"It was in a box in the basement, with about a hundred other Barbies. If we have body image issues, I know why."

I clear my throat. "We have something we have to tell you, Emma. It's pretty bad n—"

"Mr. Pritchard died," Sarah blurts out before I can finish. She says it so quickly it comes out more like "Mr. Pritcharddied."

Emma doesn't say anything at first. She walks over to the window and looks out and is quiet for a long time. When she turns around, she's crying.

"That really sucks," she says. "I mean, really, truly, in a seriously bad way."

Sarah and I nod. Emma has summed things up pretty succinctly.

Emma goes to the table and picks up a Barbie, examining it, before dropping it to the floor. "Let's go," she says, grabbing her backpack from a chair. "We are so out of here."

"Where are we going?" Sarah asks as we scramble to catch up with Emma, who's already out the door.

"Just come on," Emma says, not bothering to turn around. "I'm parked in the teachers' lot."

Sarah and I look at each other and smile. She's parked in the teachers' lot.

Now that's the Emma we know and love.

Chapter Twenty-one

Busted

It's sort of hard to explain how I got from the art room to a cell in the Manneville jail. Even harder to explain is how Mrs. Brown got there with me. With us, that is. Me, Emma, and Sarah. Oh, and Monster.

I guess I'll also need to explain how Monster got involved too.

This could be tough.

But first, let me report on the coolness of walking out to the teachers' parking lot and popping into Emma's baby blue VW Bug. Just like that. No biggie.

"I can't believe you parked here!" Sarah said when we reached the car. "Aren't you afraid of getting towed?"

"I always park here after lunch," Emma said, unlocking the passenger-side door. "The security guards never check after fifth period. It's a lot easier to get out at the end of the day."

I ducked into the backseat. "So where did you say we were going?" I asked, clicking on my seat belt, trying to sound cool. I'd never skipped school before and was acting like it was no big deal, even though my heart was thumping a million beats a minute. I felt a little bit like a crazed rabbit.

"I didn't say," Emma told me. "But I need your help getting there."

Mr. Pritchard's house wasn't that far from the high school, but it was easy to miss if you weren't looking for it, a little cottage tucked back on two acres off a back road. A FOR SALE sign was stuck in the front yard, but no one had done much to draw potential buyers in. Mr. Pritchard still owned it, but it had been a long time since he'd been able to care for it. He hadn't been planning on moving, and when a stroke landed him in the nursing home, no one had immediately jumped in to keep the house up. The grass hadn't been cut in ages, and the garden was a big, tangled mess of weeds and marigolds in full-scale rebellion.

No one had taken down the yard art, either—the huge cross covered in morning glories. Fifty years ago it had been stuck in the middle of the front yard, doused with gasoline, and lit on fire. It was still pretty scary-looking, even if there were flowers growing all over it.

"I don't think I could have lived with that thing every

day," Sarah said as we walked up the gravel driveway toward the house. "It's creepy."

Emma agreed. "It's a nightmare, right here in broad daylight. But I can see why he kept it. It was like telling the Klan, 'Bring it on, boys!'"

"So what are we doing here, anyway?" I stopped to dig a rock out of my shoe. "I'm pretty sure the house is locked."

"I just wanted to see it. I mean, I'd read about it, you know. Your dad wrote a great article."

"You read my dad's article? The one in *Southern Cultures*?"

Emma nodded. "I subscribe."

"You subscribe to *Southern Cultures*?"

"I subscribe to everything," Emma said with a shrug. "I like to know what people are thinking about."

That's when I realized something, something big. Emma was wild, all right, but she wasn't wild in the way I'd always thought she was. I'd let the biker boyfriend and the broken curfews get in the way of seeing that Emma's wildness wasn't in her actions.

It was in her brain.

We sat on the porch for a while, sometimes getting up to peek through the windows into the empty house. It was a peaceful place to be, and after a few minutes I stopped feeling nervous about skipping. We were doing something important, after all. We were honoring Mr. Pritchard.

We were living large.

It was Sarah's idea to go to Mrs. Brown's. "I bet she doesn't know about Mr. Pritchard yet," she said. "It would be awful if she found out by reading it in the paper."

So we got back in the Bug and drove to Manneville Heights, where we found Mrs. Brown out in her yard, trimming the grass along the front walk with a pair of embroidery scissors.

"Lend me a hand, dear," she said to Emma, then rose to her feet with a groan. "I hate to think my gardening days are nearing an end, but sooner or later I'm going to spend the night in my yard because none of my neighbors were outside to help me get up."

Mrs. Brown brushed a few grass clippings off her pants and then peered at us over her glasses. "The former teacher in me is wondering why you three aren't in school. It can't be later than one thirty."

That's when Emma delivered the bad news.

It was Mrs. Brown's idea to go to the farmhouse. "Harlan's the one who's held the deed to it all these years," she told us in the Bug as we drove into town, convertible top up because Mrs. Brown didn't want her hair mussed. "He doesn't have any children, so it will go to his nieces and nephews, and I imagine they'll sell it. The land's quite valuable. We should take a last look while the farmhouse is still standing."

I suppose it's possible, looking back on what happened next, that we overreacted. Or, more to the point, Sarah overreacted. She'd spent most of Sunday making plans to turn that old farmhouse into a museum, and now suddenly she had to deal with the news that it might be sold, most likely to be torn down, so that something new could be built in its place.

"If they sell it, I'll buy it," Sarah proclaimed as the car neared the soccer field.

"With what money?" Emma asked. "I bet that land goes for thousands of dollars an acre, maybe more."

"I'll think of something," Sarah insisted. "I'll contact the Historic Preservation Society." She leaned toward Mrs. Brown in the front seat. "Do you know if Manneville has a Historic Preservation Society?"

"Yes, I believe it does," Mrs. Brown assured her. "Though if I were you, I'd start filling out paperwork now. Getting a place declared a historical site can take a good while, I understand. You may not have enough time."

"I'll find the time," Sarah said, which didn't make much sense and was probably the first hint that Sarah was becoming unhinged.

We walked from the parking lot to the soccer fields, where workers from the town's Parks and Rec crew were picking up trash after Saturday soccer games. A couple of them stared at us as we cut across a field, but Emma just waved and called out, "Hey, boys! Nice weather!" and they went back to work.

We had to cross a rickety bridge over a creek to get to the farmhouse. "There used to be a much sturdier bridge here," Mrs. Brown recalled as she carefully made her way across. "Harlan built it. He loved building things. I'm glad he had his law degree, but I'm sure he would have been just as happy being a carpenter."

I recognized the farmhouse immediately. It was one of those buildings you look at all your life and never really see, just a small house with a wraparound porch and peeling white paint. A bunch of the front windows were broken, and the stairs leading up to the porch had mostly rotted away.

"Oh, how sad," Mrs. Brown said, shaking her head as we stood in the front yard looking at it. "I suppose a house can't be left alone very long before it starts falling down around itself."

Sarah stepped gingerly onto the porch and peered into one of the windows. "It looks like people have been partying in here," she reported. "I see a bunch of beer cans and some graffiti on the wall." She tried the front door, but it was locked. "They must be getting in through a window somewhere."

Emma and I took a few steps back to get a better look at the second story. Sure enough, the window on the far left was open about a foot. The better to sneak a couple of six-packs in, my dear.

"So, are you game?" Emma said, turning to me. "Ready for a little climbing action?"

I checked out the porch, the roof, the window. "I think it's going to take a ladder to get up there."

"Or a boost," Emma said. "Maybe if you climbed up on my shoulders."

"I'll do it," Sarah called over. "I'll climb through the window, take pictures with my cell phone, and begin the documentation process."

This girl will be president one day, mark my words.

If I hadn't been terrified that someone was going to end up with a broken neck, I would have found the sight of Sarah hopping up on Emma's back piggyback style and trying to get a foothold on her shoulders hilarious. It was like watching a circus act where two clumsy clowns try—and keep failing—to pull off a big stunt. But at the circus, the clowns surprise you at the last minute by pulling it off.

The only surprise here was that Sarah didn't bust a kneecap when she toppled to the ground after two seconds of teetering on top of her sister's back.

"Well, that's a bummer," she said, wiping the dirt off her pants. "But I wouldn't have been high enough up to reach the roof, anyway. What we need is somebody really tall."

We all turned and looked at Mrs. Brown, who immediately started shaking her head and backing away from us. "Oh, no, girls, don't even think about it. I'm eighty-four years old, and I am not sacrificing my back, not even for the best of causes."

Emma scratched her chin. "Well, we don't have a ladder, and the only person here tall enough to help is wisely refusing. Where does that leave us?"

"We have to get in," Sarah insisted. "If we don't, this place will be a McDonald's by next week."

Emma, Mrs. Brown, and I all looked at the farmhouse, and then we looked at Sarah. "Okay," Sarah admitted. "Maybe not a McDonald's. The access from the main road isn't good enough. But you know what I mean. A McMansion at the very least."

"What we need is somebody really tall and really strong," I said, stating the obvious. "Like a football player. Or LeBron James."

A grin broke out across Emma's face. "Give me your cell," she said to Sarah. "I know just who to call."

Chapter Twenty-two

The Jailhouse Blues

"So tell me again what this person named Monster was doing pushing Sarah into the window of an old abandoned house?"

My mom and I are sitting in the office of one Sergeant Wendell Treadway, and I'm trying to explain exactly how I ended up in the pokey.

"Sarah needed to get inside to take pictures," I say slowly. This is the third time I've told my mom the story, and she's still not getting it. I think the shock of seeing me in a jail cell has temporarily scrambled her brains. "The house might get torn down at any minute, so she had to work fast."

"Did it occur to anyone that you could have called me or your dad? We could have helped you find out how to contact Mr. Pritchard's family to discuss the matter with them. Did that occur to you?"

I take this moment to examine the WANTED poster on the wall behind my mom's head. "No, not exactly," I tell her, eying a shady-looking character named Bob Stockfish, wanted for armed robbery in fourteen states. Fourteen states? Was this guy good or what? "I guess we were just kind of caught up in the moment."

"So you decide to break into the house, but because no one can climb up on the roof, you call this Monster person—"

"Monster's his name, Mom," I interrupt. "You're saying 'Monster' like it's an adjective."

"So you call Monster," my mom revises. "And he comes and boosts Sarah up so she can climb through the window and get into the house."

"To take pictures," I remind her. "She wasn't planning on stealing anything."

My mom sighs. "And then Sarah unlocks the door from the inside, and you all go in."

"Right, and we look around, and it's so cool, because Mrs. Brown found some old record books stuffed away in a closet that listed people's names and what skills they needed to learn. Emma wants to do an oral history project, contact people who were students, the ones who are still alive, anyway—"

My mom holds up her hand. "Slow down. So tell me what happened when the police arrived."

Hmmmm. That's when things got complicated, and it's hard to sort it all out. We were in the house, going through the notebooks, and Emma started talking to Mrs. Brown about her oral history project idea, and Sarah was running from room to room with her phone, taking pictures, and I was trying to explain everything to Monster, when there was a sudden knock on the door, and a big, loud voice yelled out, "Police!"

"Don't let them in!" Sarah yelled from upstairs. "I'm not done yet! Bar the door! Board up the windows!"

Mrs. Brown opened the door. "Hello, officers. How can I help you?"

A short, stocky policeman stood on the porch with a walkie-talkie in his hand. Behind him, also in a crisp blue uniform, was the apparent winner of an Ichabod Crane look-alike contest. "You're trespassing, ma'am," the short officer told Mrs. Brown. "We just got a call from the grounds crew, saying a group of hooligans were partying out here."

Mrs. Brown raised an eyebrow. "Do I look like a hooligan to you, sir?"

"No, ma'am," the officer replied. "You don't. But you are nonetheless trespassing on private property."

"I am Mrs. Septima Brown." She pulled herself to her full height, which must have been close to six feet tall. "This is my school, young man. I'm no trespasser."

The policeman turned to the officer behind him. "Radio Joe at City and see who this house belongs to."

I think everything would have been fine if Sarah hadn't suddenly rushed out on the porch, pulled Mrs. Brown into the house, slammed the front door shut, and locked it.

"We'll come out when we're finished what we're doing!" she yelled through the closed door. "And not one second before!"

When my mom hears this, she shakes her head in disbelief. "Sarah? Sarah slammed the door on the police?"

"Well, Mrs. Brown made her open it back up. But the officer was so mad, he arrested us."

"And put you in jail? That's what I don't understand."

"He said we were resisting arrest."

"Were you?"

I shake my head. "But he was pretty mad at that point. As you might imagine."

Sergeant Treadway taps on the open door to let us know he's back. "You ladies doing okay in here?"

We both nod, but my mom shoots me a fast look that says, *We aren't done yet, missy.*

"Well, I believe your friend, Mr. Monroe, has gotten the story all straightened out for us, and Officer Rose admits that he may have overreacted after having the door slammed in his face. No charges will be pressed, and you ladies are free to go. That leaves us with just one problem."

"What's that, Sergeant?" my mom asks in her polite but tough former journalist voice.

"Well, Mrs. Brown seems disinclined to leave her jail cell. Says it's about time she did her time."

My mom stands and picks up her purse from the sergeant's desk. "Would you like us to talk to her, Sergeant Treadway?"

Sergeant Treadway looks relieved. "Would you mind? There's a concert at the university tonight, some big rock show at the Dome, which means the drunks are going to be piling up. We're really going to need that cell space come around eleven p.m."

Mrs. Brown is sitting on the bed in her cell, her purse in her lap. She is smiling. "Oh, good, I was hoping you might stop by! I wanted to let you know that I'm spending the night and you're not to bail me out. Please don't even consider it."

"But Mrs. Brown," I protest, "you're not under arrest. You're free to go."

"If I refuse to go, they'll have to arrest me for that," she says. "One way or another I'm staying. In honor of Harlan. And Martin and Medgar and Fannie Lou Hamer." She looks at me. "Do you know who Fannie Lou Hamer was?"

I shake my head. But my mom says, "Mrs. Hamer testified in front of Congress in 1963 about how she was treated in jail in Mississippi. She was a leader of the Student Nonviolent Coordinating Committee and was a hero of the civil rights movement."

I stare at her.

Mrs. Brown laughs and claps her hands. "Exactly right! Now, why doesn't everybody know that?" She leans toward us and whispers, "I'm thinking about starting another school."

"To teach literacy?" I ask.

"No, to teach children who Fannie Lou Hamer was. That's what I shall think about tonight as I sit here in my cell."

"May we bail you out in the morning?" my mother asks.

"Certainly, my dear." Mrs. Brown smiles. "I would appreciate it."

She begins to hum, and the strains of "Go Down, Moses" follow us down the hallway.

Emma and Sarah are standing with their parents outside the police station. Monster is over by the curb, talking on his cell phone. He waves when he sees me and my mom walking down the front steps.

"So this is the famous Monster," my mom whispers. "He's cute, in a gigantic sort of way."

Then she turns to the Lymans. "Henry, Ella, fancy meeting you here!"

Mr. and Mrs. Lyman dissolve into a puddle of apologies. "We don't know how— You know Emma, she's always been— I have no idea what came over Sarah— We just couldn't be more—"

My mom waves off their ditherings. "I think it's wonderful, the girls' interest in the Freedom School. Maybe they got a little carried away, sure, but I love that they're passionate about something important."

Sarah beams at my mom. Emma winks at me. Mr. and Mrs. Lyman continue to look uncomfortable as they hustle their daughters to their car, which is parked on the corner.

"Do you think they're grounded?" my mom asks.

"For life, at least," I tell her. "Maybe longer."

Monster comes over to where we're standing. "I hate to bother y'all, but do you think you could give me a ride back to my truck? I called Granny to come get me, but she's got a hot game of Hearts going at the senior center."

My mom smiles. "We'd be happy to." She checks her watch, widens her eyes in alarm. "Boy, I had no idea it was so late. Why don't you come over for dinner, uh, Monster? You guys have had a long afternoon. You must be starving."

"I could eat," Monster admits.

My mom turns to me and wiggles her eyebrows. I shrug and raise up my hands, as if to say, *What? What's all the eyebrow wiggling about?* My mom smiles as if to say, *You know exactly what all the eyebrow wiggling is about.* I shake my head vehemently to imply, *No, no, I don't know what all the eyebrow wiggling is about, and furthermore I don't* want *to know what all the eyebrow wiggling is about.*

Monster looks confused. "Is there something y'all need to tell me?"

"No!" I exclaim in a much too loud voice. I turn down the volume several notches. "I mean, not really."

"Oh, I'm just being silly," my mom tells him. "It's not every day I get to bail my firstborn out of jail."

"It's a landmark occasion," Monster agrees.

"Come on, guys, let's go eat," my mom says, and begins walking toward the car. "Monster, how do you feel about chopping off the head of a chicken?"

"Uh—" Monster suddenly looks a little green.

"Just kidding." My mom laughs. "I was actually thinking we'd have pesto."

Monster looks at me. "And I thought my people were strange."

"At least they don't blog," I tell him.

Chapter Twenty-three

Loretta Lynn: A Love Story

Monster and Loretta Lynn develop a thing for each other right away.

"I like a goat with personality," Monster tells me, rubbing Loretta Lynn on her big Roman nose. "A goat that likes a good time. A lot of goats you meet, they're way too serious."

"They've got a lot on their minds," I agree.

My mom is in the kitchen, pureeing basil and pine nuts for the pesto. My dad and Avery are in the barn, tending to the chickens. Monster, for reasons beyond my capacity to understand, has volunteered to help me milk the goats.

"I thought I'd start with goats and then work my way up to cows," he tells me. "And then maybe a moose."

"I've never heard of moose milk," I say, pulling my milking stool into place for him. "Sounds yummy."

"It's big in Japan," Monster informs me. He lowers himself onto the stool and starts sweet-talking Loretta Lynn, which I've explained to him is necessary if he's going to get a good milk haul. "Now, you are one fine goat," he murmurs into her ear. "I ain't ever seen a goat as pretty as you."

Loretta Lynn nuzzles Monster's neck. She's clearly smitten. After Monster gets into the rhythm of milking her, he looks up at me and grins.

"You know, you really are something," he says. "Only a freshman and already a B and E charge to your name, and on top of that you have your very own herd of goats. You got a lot of potential."

"For what? Becoming an A-number-one goat herder?"

"Well, that and a major felon."

I smile sweetly. "Gosh, gee, Monster, thanks."

Monster returns to his milking. After a few minutes pass, he gives Loretta Lynn one last squeeze and then stands to present me with a bucket of goat's milk. "You'd think I was born and raised on a farm, now, wouldn't you?"

"You sure would," I agree.

And then suddenly Monster is leaning toward me. He's smiling. He puts a hand on my shoulder. He looks me in the eye.

I feel myself start to panic. What's happening? What do

I want to happen? Butterflies swoosh around my stomach as I consider the possibilities.

Me and Monster?

Is that what I've wanted all along?

I flash back suddenly to eighth grade and Marc Roberts, my eighth-grade crush. He had short brown hair that always needed combing, and wore striped T-shirts that made him look like a little kid. I liked him because he was smart and funny, and different from the other eighth-grade boys. He didn't snap bra straps or huddle with his friends in the hallways and rate the girls as they walked by. Mostly you'd see him reading or hanging out with his longtime best friend, Christian Moore.

Nothing ever happened with me and Marc Roberts. When Sarah hinted around that I might like it if he asked me to the eighth-grade dance, he told her he was going to Washington, DC, with his parents that weekend, to visit the National Air and Space Museum at the Smithsonian. That was the kind of boy Marc Roberts was. That was what I liked about him, really—that he was still a boy. The other eighth-grade boys I knew were on their way to becoming something else. Criminals. Fraternity brothers. Humongous pains in the butt.

Looking up at Monster, it occurs to me that he's on his way to becoming a grown-up. He has his own apartment, a job, a truck. He's tall and powerful, kind and a little wild, but in a good, bighearted way.

He is—I realize, standing next to my favorite goat in the world—way too much for me.

Still, we stand there staring into each other's eyes like we just can't stop.

And then Monster stops. He blinks, takes a step back. Says, "You know, if you were a couple years older, I'd probably fall in love with you."

I nod my head. "Me too."

The kiss is short and very sweet. We step away from each other.

"We can still play rock and roll together, though," Monster promises me. "That don't have to change."

"And we'll always have Paris," I reply.

We walk toward the back door, swinging the bucket of milk between us. I imagine one day in the future, when the difference in our ages won't seem like such a big deal. Mr. Pritchard was eight years older than Mrs. Pritchard, after all, I remind myself.

I hope they're together somewhere right now. Maybe they're on the front porch of their old house, looking out across the wild abundance of their yard, remembering how the morning glories climbed the burnt cross every spring, how just by leaving it there and letting nature take its course, they'd turned it into art.

That's when it occurs to me to wonder: What will happen to the cross after the house is sold?

And that's when I get that feeling again, the feeling that I want to do something—something meaningful. Something *big*.

"When my dad drives you over to get your truck, I'm going too," I tell Monster, opening the back door for him. "I need you to take me somewhere."

"The prom?" Monster asks. "'Cause I gotta tell you, my tux is at the cleaners, and I got two left feet."

"Somewhere a lot more interesting than the prom," I promise.

"Consider me intrigued," comes Monster's reply.

By the time Monster and I get to Mr. Pritchard's house, it's almost nine o'clock, and the sky is blazing with stars. The cross stands in the moonlight, the brown vines of faded morning glories still clinging to it.

"So I guess you're wondering why I brought a couple of shovels," I say to Monster as we climb out of the truck. "In fact, I bet you're wondering what we're doing here at all."

"Considering that I've asked you seventeen times since we left your house, that's a pretty safe bet," Monster replies, reaching into the truck bed to get out our tools.

I point to the cross. "We're going to dig that up and take it back to my house."

When Monster's eyes land on the cross, he takes a few steps back. "Man, I got to warn you, them Baptists get mean when you start digging up their holy relics."

"This isn't a church," I tell him. "It's Mr. Pritchard's house. That's the cross the Klan burned. He left it there. But as soon as his house gets sold, the new owners will take it down probably. They won't understand that it's art."

"They'll probably put in a few lawn gnomes instead," Monster agrees. "Not that you can necessarily blame 'em. That's a pretty powerful statement to have to mow around every Saturday."

We walk over to the cross, which has to be at least ten feet tall. I look up at it and feel a shiver go through me. "Is it sacrilege to dig up a cross?" I ask, starting to have doubts about what we're going to do. "Or, I don't know, weird?"

Monster considers this for a moment. "Well, it's gonna get dug up one way or another, right? Probably by a real estate agent now that Mr. Pritchard's gone and don't have a say in it. A burnt cross on the lawn ain't exactly a selling point. So it'll get dug up and thrown into a dump truck, and dumped into the landfill. That seems a lot more sacrilegious to me than us digging it up and making some kind of memorial out of it."

And so we begin to dig.

I don't know how much time you've spent digging up a ten-foot burnt cross from somebody's front yard, but I'm here to tell you, it takes a while. Five minutes into it, I'm seriously regretting that I didn't bring gloves. I can feel the blisters rising in painful little relief maps all over my palms.

"You know, if you were really my friend, you'd tell me to take a break while you finish up," I tell Monster, leaning against my shovel and breathing hard. "I think I forgot to mention that I'm a delicate flower."

"Well, you smell good," Monster agrees, still digging. "But you throw around a bass too easy for me to think you can't do a little yard work when the situation calls for it."

He's right. I've only been playing bass a few weeks and you can already see the change in my biceps. I start digging again.

It takes us forty-five minutes to dig through the rocky ground and carefully pull out the cross and lay it on the yard. I kneel beside it and put my hand on a burned place. It feels evil to me.

"Only one thing to do about hate that big," Monster says, pulling my hand away so it's no longer touching the dark spot. "And that's to put a bigger love out there. Like your friend Mr. Pritchard did."

"And Mrs. Pritchard," I add. "And Mrs. Brown."

"Big love, dude," Monster says, pulling me up. "Beats big hate every time."

We haul the cross to the truck and carefully lift it into the back.

And so ends the strangest and maybe most amazing day

of my life, with me and Monster driving down the road in the dark, a burnt cross in the truck bed behind us, the two of us singing along with the radio to a song I don't even know the words to, and I don't even care. I just keep singing.

Chapter Twenty-four

Field of Dreams

Some girls are presented at debutante balls. Others are bat mitzvahed. Lucky Korean girls have a *Gwallye* ceremony to celebrate their coming of age.

Me, I get a hootenanny.

God bless America.

The hootenanny of all hootenannies takes place tonight, and my birthday is tomorrow. My fifteenth birthday.

"Your *Quinceañera*," my mom informs me this morning. "The funny thing is, when I started planning the hootenanny, I didn't put two and two together. I knew the hootenanny would be on Saturday and your birthday was the next day, but the fact that you're turning fifteen just hit me last night. That's a special birthday for a girl."

"Yes, if the girl happens to be Hispanic or Latina," I tell her. "But, sadly, I am neither."

We're sitting at the breakfast table eating French toast,

and because the sun didn't rise until 7:10, it isn't even that absurdly early to be up and at 'em. Not that I wouldn't prefer to be snug as a bug up in my bed, mind you, but you take what you can get when you live in Farm World.

My mom leans back and takes a sip of coffee. "So, how should we celebrate this milestone birthday of yours?"

"By not having a hootenanny?" I suggest.

"Not have the hootenanny?" My mom looks aghast. "Honey, it's going to be the social event of the year. And all your friends will be there—Sarah and Emma, Monster, Virginia—"

"Verbena," I correct her.

"And I invited Mrs. Brown and Monster's grandmother and all the ladies from the quilting circle."

"And don't forget Mrs. Welsch," I remind her. "The Agrarian Librarian."

My mom spikes a piece of French toast from my plate. "It's a shame about that rat eating her chicken. But I've promised her one of our Faverolles hens. Those girls are big."

I take one last swig of orange juice and stand. "Well, I've got some goats to tend to, if you'll excuse me."

"What about your *Quinceañera*?" my mom calls after me.

"We could have it in Mexico City," I call back over my shoulder as I take to the stairs. "Where it would actually make sense and be semi-appropriate."

After pulling on my Farm World jeans and "Rednecks for Peace" T-shirt, I hurry out to the goat pen. There's a lot to talk about, and Loretta Lynn is just the girl—er, goat—to talk to. I don't even mind the fact that Patsy Cline and Kitty Wells are clearly eavesdropping.

"So you'll be happy to know that the presentation was a huge hit," I tell Loretta Lynn as I clean out the straw that's gotten into her water. "The best part was when we had Mrs. Brown come in and talk. Did I tell you that we broadened our topic to include Mrs. Brown, not just Hazel Pritchard?"

Loretta Lynn widens her eyes. This is news to her.

"Yeah, so we did," I continue. "I mean, it only seemed right. The Freedom School was her idea, after all. And Emma helped us set up a multimedia presentation, so we had Sarah's pictures of the school, and Mr. Pritchard talking to my dad about Mrs. Pritchard, and film footage of the Pritchards' yard. It was really cool."

Loretta Lynn bleats in an inquiring sort of way.

"Of course we got an A," I tell her. "Do you even have to ask? By the end of our presentation, Ms. Morrison and Marley Baxter were both crying. It was really cool. And after class was over, Wallace asked Sarah out, and she said yes."

Patsy Cline and Kitty Wells butt heads at this news. Frankly, it was a shock to me, too. I didn't even know Wallace had the gift of speech. But as it turns out, once he opens his mouth, he's actually a very articulate guy.

"So what kind of phone do you have?" he asked Sarah. "Those pictures of the school you took were awesome."

The conversation took off from there, and before you knew it, Wallace had offered to escort Sarah to the city council meeting on Wednesday. As it just so happens, he always attends city council meetings and is more than willing to guide Sarah through the ins and outs of local politics.

It would appear to be a match made in heaven.

"And then guess who was waiting for me at my locker after class?" I ask Loretta, who smirks at me, as though she knows exactly who was waiting for me.

"No, it wasn't Monster," I tell her, matching her smirk for smirk. "It was Jeremy Fitch."

That shuts her up.

It shut me up too. I'd thought Jeremy Fitch was a part of the story that was over. He'd been a fun fantasy crush, but a dud in real life, and besides, I didn't have any interest in being a member of his fan club. So when I saw him waiting for me at my locker, I was a little taken aback. It was like reading *Twilight* and suddenly Harry Potter shows up in Chapter Eight. What was he doing there?

"You going to Jam Band today?" Jeremy asked, casually leaning against the locker next to mine. "I could give you a ride home."

"How much would it cost me?"

Jeremy grinned his charming grin. "Oh, that. I was just freaking out that day. My dad told me the night before I was going to have to get a job to pay for my own insurance and gas. Sorry I was so uncool."

I waited for him to give me my five dollars back.

He didn't.

"So, anyway," he continued after an uncomfortable silence. "You need a ride?"

"I'm skipping Jam Band today," I told him, grabbing my algebra book and shoving it into my backpack. "My mom's got this big party tomorrow, and I have to help her get ready."

"Oh, yeah, I heard about that. Sounds like a lot of guys from Jam Band are going. Am I invited too?"

I was tempted to tell him no. I was tempted to explain to him that all fall Sarah and I had had a huge crush on him, but then he'd shown his true colors and the spell had been broken, and even if I didn't have a boyfriend or even a crush, Monster and Todd had shown me that a girl shouldn't just settle for anyone, and besides, Jeremy wasn't half the man Monster was, and quite frankly, I'd rather not see his sorry butt at my mom's hootenanny—

And then Monster came up behind Jeremy and slapped his back and said, "Hey, how's it going, dude?"

Which is when I remembered that Jeremy was Monster's

friend, and I guessed any friend of Monster's was a friend of mine.

"Sure you're invited," I told him. "Maybe Monster could give you a ride, save you some gas money."

Jeremy winked at me. "Great idea."

Wow, what had Sarah and I been thinking?

"So I guess I'll try to be friends with Jeremy," I tell Loretta Lynn, who's licking the last of the grain from her lips. "But do I want to go out with him? I think not."

In the two weeks since Monster and I shared our brief kiss, I've given a lot of thought to who I'd like to go out with, but I remain uninspired. Verbena wants me to hook up with someone from Jam Band now that she and Jason are an item, but the black T-shirt thing gets old after a while. Besides, I still can't help but think of Marc Roberts, my eighth-grade crush. Smart, cute, nice—and, well, okay, normal.

Just like I used to be.

"You mean boring," Verbena had said at lunch on Friday, when I mentioned Marc to her. We eat in the cafeteria most days now, but usually spend the last ten minutes of lunch period in the library, for old times' sake. Jason joins us, even though the library isn't really, as he puts it, his scene. He occasionally offers a quote from a song to underline someone's point, a bit of Led Zeppelin lyric or a piece of Jack White wisdom, but for the most part doodles on his arm with his Sharpie and doesn't say much at all, except to protest when Verbena grabs the Sharpie away for her own doodles.

They are clearly a couple in need of his 'n' hers Sharpies.

"I *don't* mean boring," I told Verbena, popping an M&M into my mouth just to see if Mrs. Welsch will pounce on me. But ever since our talk about where to keep chicken feed, Mrs. Welsch has adopted a live-and-let-live attitude and hasn't shushed me once.

I always knew that underneath it all she was good people.

"This Marc Roberts guy sounds outrageously boring," Verbena insists. "And way too young. I don't know why you and Monster don't give in to your passion."

"Because Monster has his own apartment," I tell her. "I'm not ready for a man with an apartment."

"I am," Verbena purrs, nudging Jason with her elbow.

Jason looks up from his doodling, startled. "My mom won't let me get my own apartment. She still makes me share a room with my little brother."

Verbena sighs.

"I just want someone normal," I tell Verbena. "No apartments, no Romeo games, just a nice, normal guy."

Verbena looks me straight in the eye. "Oh, Janie, you are so past normal. Normal was ten miles ago and in another county."

I've been thinking about what Verbena said ever since.

I think about it when I look at my collage, which is leaning against the barn. It's not the collage I originally planned—the quartz, the parasol, the cutout words, the sketch of Mr. and Mrs. Pritchard. I made that collage, and it was nice. Ms. Ashdown declared it a perfectly fine first effort.

"But I know you can do better," she told me, peering at me over her cat's-eye glasses. "I know you can do something bigger."

I think she meant "bigger" as in "conceptually bigger," but I did her one better. I went all-out big. I went large.

I went *huge.*

It's not a collage exactly, not the way you normally think about collage. Call it found art. Call it Rauschenberg-esque. When Ms. Ashdown drove out to see it, she called it postmodern—right before she gave it an A.

"But where did you find that cross?" she asked. "It's beautiful—and kind of terrifying."

So I told her the story of Mr. and Mrs. Pritchard—and Mrs. Brown and the Freedom School.

"And so you've put the cross on its side?" Ms. Ashdown asked, walking closer to the barn, where I'd leaned the cross and made a kind of garden around it—a border of rocks from the Pritchards' yard, and some rosemary I'd found growing in Mrs. Pritchard's herb garden.

"It makes an *X* that way," I explained, but by the way

Ms. Ashdown raised one eyebrow, I could tell she didn't quite get it.

"That's how people who can't read or write sign their names." I gestured for Ms. Ashdown to come closer. "But see those pieces of paper shellacked to the cross? Mrs. Brown let me use some of the stuff from the notebooks we found stored in the school. So that right there"—I pointed to a scrap with MARY SIMMONS written across it in an unsteady cursive—"is from Mrs. Simmons's notebook, and there's where George Whisnant practiced his signature, and over there, that's Cletus Miller's."

Next weekend Monster is coming over with his truck, and we're moving the cross over to the Freedom School. Mr. Pritchard's nephew, Philip, a civil rights lawyer in Atlanta, deeded the old house to Mrs. Brown, who continues to work on her plans to make Fannie Lou Hamer a household name. Emma's helping her, and so is my mom. When the Freedom School reopens in the spring, Sarah and I are going to tutor kids in reading.

When I think about everything that's happened since school started, well, I don't think the word "normal" applies to any of it. Verbena is right—I'm way past normal. Only I've realized that when you move beyond normal, the road you're on doesn't necessarily take you to the land of the abnormal or the weird or the freakish. Instead you might find yourself in a place where people build Freedom Schools and have the courage to live large.

It's a place where people don't worry too much when they get a little goat poop on their shoes.

Around six forty-five my mom starts to get seriously anxious. The hootenanny starts at seven—but what if no one shows up? "I'll feel like a hoote*ninny* if nobody comes," she declares, which cracks Avery up so much she gets the hiccups. We spend five minutes pouring glasses of water down her throat and jumping out from behind the door in an attempt to scare the hiccups away.

By the time things have settled down, it's 6:50, and the first set of headlights appears on the horizon, followed by what appears to be a wagon train of minivans and pickup trucks. Someone's high beams catch the cross leaning against the side of the barn.

I hope people go up and take a close look at it. I hope they read the names.

My dad puts an arm around my mom's shoulder and says, "You better get your fiddle tuned up. Looks like it's going to be a hoedown, pardner."

The great big irony of this hootenanny? My mom doesn't actually play an instrument. She just likes the idea of a hundred other people sitting around playing instruments while she listens.

Normal so clearly does not run in my family.

By nine o'clock, Sarah and Emma have become the stars of the show. They are backed by the Jam Band and the Manneville Ukulele Orchestra as they lead everyone in a rousing version of "Sunrise, Sunset" from *Fiddler on the Roof.* I'm standing at the edge of the crowd, taking it all in, when Monster comes up beside me, his hands behind his back.

"Why aren't you playing with the Jam Band?" I ask, trying to sneak a peek to see what he's holding—because he's definitely holding something.

"I was, but your mom asked me to do her a favor. So if you'll just close your eyes . . ."

I laugh, but Monster insists. "Shut 'em tight. I got something that I need to present to you. And you oughta thank me, because I talked your mom out of doing it in front of the whole party."

I shut my eyes tight. "I'll do whatever you say."

Monster places something on my head. I reach up to feel it. Whatever it is, it's sharp and pointy. "What's up there?" I ask. "Can I look?"

I open my eyes. Monster's grinning. "Happy *Quinceañera,* big girl."

The crown I pull off my head looks like something out of *Snow White,* beautiful and shiny, encrusted with all sorts of fake jewels that sparkle in the party lights strung across the barn.

"Your mom made it," Monster informs me. "She said it took her all week."

"No way!" I exclaim. "My mom couldn't make this. This is way beyond her."

"She said she ruined four sweaters in the attempt."

"Well, that does sound like her creative process," I admit.

Suddenly I hear my name called from across the distance. It's Sarah and Emma. Emma is holding up my bass.

Monster pushes me forward. "Go on, birthday girl. Show 'em your stuff."

"You come too," I tell him, suddenly feeling nervous and a little embarrassed, picturing myself in front of a crowd of mostly strangers, playing bass and wearing a fake diamond-encrusted crown.

"It ain't my birthday," he says, but he takes my hand and gives me his big Monster grin, and off we go for a little klezmer birthday fun.

Normal, in case you were wondering, is vastly overrated.

Also by Frances O'Roark Dowell

Dovey Coe

Where I'd Like to Be

The Secret Language of Girls

Chicken Boy

Shooting the Moon

The Kind of Friends We Used to Be

Falling In

THE PHINEAS L. MacGUIRE BOOKS
(Illustrated by Preston McDaniels)

Phineas L. MacGuire . . . Erupts!

Phineas L. MacGuire . . . Gets Slimed!

Phineas L. MacGuire . . . Blasts Off!